*THEY HAD BREAKFAST IN BED,
SERVED BY A CYBERBUTLER.*

Chane ate ravenously while listening to Lizina's plan for revenge. "You're a total lunatic," he said. "Mad as a rabid grat. But you'll try it whether I'm here or not."

Before she could protest, Chane continued. "No point sitting around while you get yourself killed—so I might as well help you."

Lizina shrieked with joy and flung her arms around him, upsetting the breakfast tray. Chane returned the embrace—and more. "Is this the way I'm supposed to earn that exorbitantly high salary you've promised me?"

Lizina matched his motion with her own. "This is just a (uh!) fringe benefit, guaranteed to promote a better employee/employer relationship. *Ohh.*"

SPACEWAYS

SPACEWAYS #7

THE MANHUNTRESS
JOHN CLEVE

PLAYBOY PAPERBACKS

QALARA

RAHMAN

THE CARNADYNE VOID

THE CORSI CLUSTER

BLEAK

SKYLLA
KARYBDIS

LUHRA

FRANJI

AGLAYA

MURPH

TERASAKI

FRONT

NEVERMIND

SHIRASH

THE MAELSTROM

OUTREACH

THEBANIS

TRI-SYSTEM ACCORD

GHANJ

MECCAH

JASBIR

JARPI

PANISH

RESH

SAMANNA

JAHPUR

SUZI

SHANKAR

LANATIA

CROZ

HELLHOLE

SAIPING

CORSI

A: All planets are not shown.
B: Map is not to scale, because of
   the vast distances between stars.

SCARLET HILLS

Alas, fair ones, my time has come.
I must depart your lovely home—
Seek the bounds of this galaxy
To find what lies beyond.

(chorus)
Scarlet hills and amber skies,
Gentlebeings with loving eyes;
All these I leave to search for a dream
That will cure the wand'rer in me.

You say it must be glamorous
For those who travel out through space.
You know not the dark, endless night
Nor the solitude we face.

(reprise chorus)

I know not of my journey's end
Nor the time nor toll it will have me spend.
But I must see what I've never seen
And know what I've never known.

Scarlet hills and amber skies,
Gentlebeings with loving eyes;
All these I leave to search for a dream
That will cure the wand'rer in me.

—Ann Morris

A shark circled in space.

To be certain, this shark's lineage could not be traced to the flesh- and blood-eating machine that swam the oceans of now forgotten Homeworld. Nor was it biological.

It was a shark, just the same.

And it *was* an eating machine. An eater of other machines—and of men.

A sleek, finless shark, it was designed to slice through the infinitely stretching light-years of space. A shark of gleaming naked metal that bore the single marking *Lung T'ou* emblazoned in crimson along its prow.

Shark and spacer—both predators. Both preyed on the weak, the injured, and the crippled.

In an earlier age, millennia in humankind's past, *Lung T'ou* would have been constructed of wood and pitch. Its bow would have cut through the waves of Homeworld's neglected seas. Sails, hung from strong masts, would have billowed in the wind. Atop the highest of those masts would have flown a flag—skull and crossed bones on a field of jet.

Lung T'ou was a direct descendant of such a craft. The men and women who rode its decks bore the same infamous title given those who trod the decks of those wooden ships—pirates.

Like a shark that smelled blood, *Lung T'ou* circled its prey. It—or its captain—bided his time, waiting for the moment to move in for the kill.

That moment rapidly approached.

1

Through eyes that were not eyes, Dorjan of Harb scanned the control console's flashing lights, monitors, and mini-displays. Each told him something, whether he wanted to know it or not. He narrowed his three-hundred-sixty-degree telepresence vision to focus on a green phosphor screen to his left.

A trajectory readout listed down the left side of the monitor. Right of the column of figures, high resolution graphics bracketed the other spacecraft's minute course change.

"Bastard!"

Dorjan's fingers danced over a series of glo-red buttons on the console's face.

A hint of vibration ran through the deck. Maneuvering rockets ignited to synchronize the ship—his ship, *Misfit*—with the trajectory of the other, which floated twenty-five kloms out in space.

Prow facing prow, the death-dance of the two spacers had continued in a sort of slow-motion tarantella for five hours. *Lung T'ou* led; *Misfit* followed. Neither captain exposed his ship's sides to the other.

To have done so would have been instantaneous suicide for the captain making that elementary mistake in tactics.

When humankind sailed wooden ships across the oceans of Homeworld, warring vessels maneuvered for hours in an attempt to expose the cannons positioned along their great lengths to their opponents. If a vulnerable bow or stern were presented to an attacker, the ship was soon raked by a bellowing broadside.

The tactic was called crossing the T. Cap'n Harry Morgan loved it. So did once-pirate Captain John Paul Jones. And so did Captain Jonuta.

In space the name remained. With Defense Systemry located in the prows of most spacers, the tactic was reversed. To expose a side to an aggressor was to create a prime target—a broad indefensible target for forward-mounted gunnery.

Spaceships faced nose-to-nose presented smaller targets for enemy gunners (human or automated). And it was far easier to maneuver out of the line of direct fire.

So it was that *Misfit* and *Lung T'ou* danced in circles twenty-five kilometers from each other. Neither ship fired on the other.

For *Lung T'ou* there was no need to attack. *Misfit* was already crippled. A polarization cell in the spacer's double P drive had done its best to vaporize when the ship punched from the Tachyon Trail—''subspace''—for a navigation check in the Ahura Mazda System.

For *Misfit* to attack its pirate opponent would have been yet another form of suicide for Dorjan and his six crew members. *Misfit*'s tachyon propulsion system was now vulnerably open and totally useless.

Songan, *Misfit*'s massively tattooed First Mate, labored within the drive's housing to replace the disfunctioning polarization cell. Inside with him—as they had been for the past six hours—were crewmates Iniko and Hedeon.

Dorjan had only his ship's chemical maneuvering rockets at the command of his fingertips. And those . . .

''MR system check?'' Dorjan brought the mentally controlled necklace-like row of TPs inset in the skin at the base of his neck back to full three-hundred-sixty-degree scope.

"Two-minute continuous burn. Five minutes worth of short bursts. If *Lung T'ou* makes a radical change in its course . . ." Varnalgeran Yuw's answer faded in hopeless silence.

Dorjan suppressed the panic that squirmed in his gut. *Five minutes—at most! Then?*

Misfit's maneuvering rockets weren't designed for sustained use. They were meant for the precision trajectory corrections needed during docking alignment at space stations. The rockets were chemical. Depletable chemical agents. Fuel that had to be replenished each time the ship was berthed.

That they had lasted this long bordered on the miraculous.

One miracle wasn't going to be enough today. Not if Dorjan intended to save ship and crew from the circling, stalking *Lung T'ou*.

The man hunched over SIPACUM to Dorjan's right glanced at his captain. Varnalgeran Yuw's expression contained the same helplessness that had been implicit in his silence. The computrician's eye-blinking red shirt lay matted against his overweight body. Soaked with five hours of sweat. And fear!

The same sweat drenched Dorjan's own clothing. The same fear set his temples pounding as though they contained bass drums gone berserk.

The Outie's appearance provided no reassurance of Dorjan's ability to extricate ship and crew from their perilous position. Dorjan had never seen the man sweat—before. While others might crack and crumble under pressure, Varn remained cool, iceberg cool. For this native of the planet Outreach to . . .

A blip on the green monitor broke Dorjan's digression. His fingers jabbed at the console once more, matching *Misfit*'s trajectory with the pirate ship's.

"One minute, forty-five," Varn called out the time remaining to the maneuvering rockets.

Dorjan toed open intraship communications. His voice came from his throat in a harsh bark. The strain of five hours of unrelenting tension crackled through *Misfit*.

"Damn it, Songan, how much longer! I can't keep SotKil off *Misfit* forever! Stop playing with yourself and get the drive up!"

A grille hissed on the console before the master of *Misfit*. The words that crackled from the speaker sounded less than human—mechanical. They were. Years ago on Harb, Songan's vocal cords had been severed. He spoke through a voice box inset in the small of his throat like a chainless medallion of gold.

"Dorjan, if you think that you . . ."

The speaker grille went dead for a long silent moment. When Songan's voice returned, it was restrained. "The polarization cell is repaired and functioning perfectly. We need at least ten minutes for final adjustments and closing the housing."

"You've got less than five!"

Dorjan saw Varn's eyes narrow. The Outie wasn't accustomed to hearing a sharp exchange between captain and Mate. Nor did Songan deserve it. No man or woman who roamed the spaceways could ask for a better Mate than Dorjan's fellow Harbian.

The two had once been slave-gladiators on the outworld planet Harb. Both still carried permanent reminders of that former life.

For Songan those souvenirs of bondage were his tattoos (from the top of his shaven scalp to the soles of his feet with no sem between left unembellished), his genetically engineered strength, his voice box . . . and a good brain that had been encephaloboosted beyond mere genius.

Dorjan's chromosomes had also been manipulated while he had been in his mother's womb. He was a sport, a genetic freak. An albino (though his skin was now subcutaned to a deep nut brown).

As an adult he had been blinded, his vision restored via the TP/telepresences in his neck. Bioengineered wings of ultra-thin unipolymer plasteel were attached to his back. Retractable plasteel claws (each a full three sems in length) were surgically implanted to replace his fingernails. (The claw in each forefinger could become a mini vibe-knife with one conscious mental command).

The alterations of mind and body were the gifts of their former owner Murrah an Rahmyne. To Murrah the two men had been prized possessions whose bodies were to be honed to total killing machines.

Dorjan had accidentally killed Murrah. Slaves were slaves and masters were masters. The first did not kill the latter—even accidentally.

Dorjan and Songan had fled the galactic rim aboard *Misfit*—Murrah's private pleasure ship—to the star-crammed center of the Milky Way. There, among the worlds and stars humankind (whose members now bore the self-applied appellation Galactics) called the Farther Reaches, they had used *Misfit* to develop a successful freight trade.

With Songan, the captain of *Misfit* had discovered an abandoned asteroid colony in the planetless star system Pascal. A colony they reclaimed and converted into a haven for escaped slaves just such as they. The same colony they named HOME (Habitat Orbiter: Modular Environment).

For eight years they had labored to revamp HOME, transforming it into a massive ship, five kloms long and capable of exploring the stars. The colony-spacer now awaited *Misfit*'s return to begin its maiden voyage.

Financing that gargantuan conversion had given birth to another shared venture for the two ex-slaves of Harb. The creation of The Shadow Walker—master thief among the settled worlds of humankind.

Will with the Wisp, The Demon Cat, The Invisible

One, The-Thief-Who-Is-Not-There—his names were legend and so were his exploits. In truth The Shadow Walker was two people. Songan, whose intelligence had been encephaloboosted beyond genius, masterminded each of The Demon Cat's escapades. And Dorjan, the adventurer, the man who actually performed the daring thefts.*

The high resolution image of spacer *Lung T'ou* leaped upward on the green phosphor monitor. Dorjan's fingers jabbed the console. *Misfit*'s prow rose to follow the pirate ship's abrupt course change.

"MR reads one minute remaining." Yuw was repeating the figures provided by that marvelously engineered necessity of space travel: SIPACUM (Ship Inboard Processing and Computing Unit [Modular]).

Dorjan inwardly cringed. Another radical trajectory modification like the last one and *Lung T'ou* would be on *Misfit* in a manner of minutes. *Move it, Songan. Move it, damn it!*

Stuck in this barren star system far beyond the Carnadyne Void, trying to outmaneuver a pirate, was no place for a thief. Nor would Dorjan have been here, crippled in unfamiliar space, were it not for Lizina and Kefira altRusalka.

Lizina. The name evoked a tidal wave of memories. Lizina—the woman he loved. The woman who now carried his unborn child.

And Kefira. That woman of the alien Akil race was unique to the Galactic worlds. She was the only member of her race humankind had encountered. Saucereyed, furred in white gold, the sensuous Akil also held a special place in Dorjan's heart.

Both women had been under his protection when HOME was attacked by Ganesa of Resh, mistress of the spacegoing brothel *Be Lively*. Lizina and Kefira had been kidnapped by the Reshi madam.

---

* Spaceways #5: *Master of Misfit*.

After searching the Farther Reaches for months, Dorjan had caught up with Ganesa at the Barbro Transfer Station two days ago. The woman had revealed that Lizina and Kefira had been sold on the mining planets Mirjam and Ginneh, respectively. Leaving Ganesa and crew bound and gagged, Dorjan had programmed *Be Lively* for Forty Per Cent City, then escaped Barbro with a TransGalactic Watch destrier on *Misfit*'s tail.

Whether Ganesa survived the jam-cram into subspace was a question that might never be answered. The tactic, usually reserved for desperate situations, was one of the gray areas of traveling the Tachyon Trail. The probability was just above seventy per cent for survival with undefined damage and 59.7731-to-infinity per cent for survival intact. That left 40.2269 per cent probability of utter destruction, presumably.

Those who had become a part of that last statistic were not around to tell about it.

Dorjan no longer thought about Ganesa. He had given her a chance. More than she had given the fifty HOMErs butchered in *Be Lively*'s attack on the asteroid colony.

Though sold into slavery, Lizina and Kefira still lived. So long as they lived, Dorjan could hope. He clung to that hope. It was more than Songan had.

Yoluta, the young Lanatian whom Songan was to marry, had been killed in the raid on HOME. *Misfit*'s First Mate now traveled the spaceways seeking the technology needed to clone Yoluta from cell samples taken from her body by HOME's physician.

The search for three lost women had brought *Misfit* to the Ahura Mazda System. That the *Lung T'ou* had happened upon the crippled ship during the repairs of the malfunctioning polarization cell was a matter of fate.

The phosphor screen burped an emerald blip. Dorjan fed new coordinates into the console. Varnalgeran Yuw informed his captain that SIPACUM registered thirty seconds burn left to the chemical rockets.

Come on, Songan! Move your tattooed backside!

Dorjan tapped intraship comm open with the toes of his right foot. "Status?"

"Five minutes more," Songan said. "We'll be out of here in five minutes, Dorjan. Give us five *more* minutes!"

Varn shook his head as Dorjan turned to him. Songan might as well have asked for the universe on a reelsilver platter.

"Songbird: Edrek?" Dorjan checked with the two crew members who manually manned *Misfit*'s DS.

An ear-piercing *"tweet"* answered, followed by an "affirmative."

The non-human whistle belonged to Songbird, a Jarp. Songbird was neither male nor female, but both. It was hermaphroditic, possessing breasts, a penis, a testicle, and an ovary. Songbird's shockingly orange skin and deep wine-red hair were common to all natives of the planet Jarpi.

The "affirmative" was from Edrek, the youngest of *Misfit*'s crew.

Edrek had a double stake in *Misfit*'s success. Yoluta was—or had been—his sister. Kefira had been his lover since Dorjan and crew had rescued the brother and sister from slavery on the planet Thebanis.

"Stand ready," Dorjan said. "We've got one last move in us, then . . . when *Lung T'ou* tries to take us, show them we have some fight left in us."

Dorjan sensed teeth-gritted determination in the "tweet" and "affirmative" that answered his command.

"Intraship comm, captain," Varn said. "It's SotKil again."

"Bring it up—minus visual."

SotKil. Lung T'ou. The names sounded as though they had been taken from a martial arts edutape. SotKil—the

Hammer Fist. Lung T'ou—the Dragon's Head. Charming. The type of names a certain sort of man selected for sheer showmanship.

That was, if one were not from the planet Saiping. SotKill was Saipese. (Dorjan knew. He had listened to the pirate captain's demand for surrender twice an hour during the long standoff.) Saipese did not assume such names. They were given. An honor for achievement— for an outstanding attribute!

The Hammer Fist! The name rang ominously.

But then so did *Death*. And that was the name Dorjan had been given while in the arena of Harb.

"Ah, Captain Dasan, we speak once again." SotKil's voice crackled from the speaker grille. *"This time I hope you will be more amiable to my request to board* Nobigthing *and relieve your ship of the burden it carries."*

"Once again, captain, I must inform you *Nobigthing*'s holds are empty." Dorjan did his best to remain calm, to infuse a casual conversational tone in his voice. "We're en route to Mirjam seeking cargo. Not carrying."

"Captain, I grow weary of the charade. It is well-known along the spaceways that this portion of the Tachyon Trail is a main artery in the TZ trade . . ."

The only charade Dorjan played was his assumed identity of Captain Dasan and *Misfit*'s temporary registration as the spacer *Nobigthing*. For the Invisible One— master thief of the galaxy—disguise for captain, ship, and crew were essential to the continued prosperity of all.

Misfit/Nobigthing's holds *were* empty.

Were they not, Dorjan would never carry TZ—tetrazombase. The will-and-mind-robbing drug was illegal on every Galactic-settled planet along the spaceways. It was an essential tool for many slavers.

Though often on the wrong side of legality, Dorjan never engaged in the trade of flesh, human or alien.

His ten years of freedom had been dedicated to spoiling the profits of those slavers who crossed his path.

"... *I've tracked your vessel from Ginneh, captain. I grow tired of this grat and mouse game. Allow the boarding and you and your three crewmates will live. Deny me again and the four of you will spacewalk— without suits!*"

The green monitor blipped. Dorjan punched in the correcting course that kept *Misfit/Nobigthing* face-to-face with the pirate craft.

Varnalgeran Yuw raised a hand, forefinger and thumb touching. The silent signal's connotation was far from its usual meaning. The MR was depleted. Zero! There would be no more maneuvering for *Misfit*.

SotKil, the Hammer Fist, had to be reckoned with. *The Hammer Fist*.

"Captain SotKil, I assure you that you have mistaken *Nobigthing* for another spacer ..." Dorjan had said it all before. Now he repeated himself to buy time. Something SotKil had said niggled at the back of his mind.

Three!

SotKil had said *three* crew members. *Misfit* carried a captain and a crew of *six*!

How could Lung T'ou's *scans and sensors have mis-read the persons onboard* Misfit? *It made no sense. It ...*

Songan!

Dorjan almost stumbled over his words as it came to him. Songan, Iniko. and Hedeon were within the drive's housing. That housing contained half a centimeter of lead shielding.

The sensors and scans couldn't penetrate the lead. SotKil doesn't realize I've got six men onboard with me.

"... Captain SotKil, there seems to be but one way of convincing you of your mistake." Dorjan paused, trying to quell the doubt knotting his gut. He *could* be wrong. "You and your crew may board *Nobigthing*."

Varn's head jerked around. Shock filled his expression.

Dorjan toed off intraship comm, switching to intership. "Songan! You and Iniko and Hedeon stay where you are. If any of you step out of the drive housing before I give the order, I'll personally have your hides before SotKil has a chance at them.

"Varn, give me another reading on SotKil's crew. Now!"

Dorjan tapped intraship communications again. He had missed only a few words of SotKil's reply.

"*. . . you and your three crew members waiting at the airlock. Unarmed. Understand?*"

Yuw held up four fingers as Dorjan said, "Understood. We'll be waiting as requested. *Unarmed.*"

Intership comm off again, Dorjan swiveled to his computrician. "We've got ten, maybe fifteen minutes, until SotKil arrives. With luck, just enough time to prepare a suitable welcoming for the sisterslicer!"

Dorjan smiled. The Tao taught that one should meet hard with soft. And Dorjan was a Taoist, a follower of The Way.

When the Hammer Fist strikes, it will strike water. And no hammer has ever injured water!

2

Thrusting rockets ignited. Thunder reverberated within the shuttle to fold back on itself in a deafening chorus.

An invisible hand reached down and pressed itself flat against Lizina's face and chest. She offered no resistance. She relaxed and allowed the mashing force to shove her into the padding of the contour couch.

And-a-one-and-a-two-and-a-three-and-a-four-and-a-five-and-a . . .

She tried to ignore the ever-increasing pressure that sought to squeeze the breath from her lungs. The pilot had assured her the shuttle would clear Mirjam's gravity well in seventy-eight point eight-three seconds. So she counted, mentally clicking off each agonizing second of the launch.

Many of the planets within the Farther Reaches were connected to their space stations via beanstalk elevators. The counter weight of upward and downward traffic to the torus-shaped stations eliminated the brute force required to reach escape velocity under rocket power.

Mirjam was not a planet of the Farther Reaches. It was an underdeveloped mining world out beyond that eerie starless expanse called Carnadyne Void. Mirjam, despite its highly profitable copper trade, had no elevators rising into space.

Mirjam still awaited the construction of a full-fledged space station.

The shuttle's hull vibrated around its lone passenger

21

as if intent on tearing itself apart at the seams. Lizina's teeth rattled even while she did her best to clamp her jaw firmly closed.

. . .   *and-a-fifty-and-a-one-and-a-fifty-two-and-a-fifty* . . .

In the two couches ahead of her, Lizina saw the pilot's and co-pilot's hands lazily drift over the flashing array of the ship's control console. Here and there, fingertips dipped to jab and punch in multiple-gee slow motion.

Outside, beyond the shuttle's blunted nose, Mirjam's pale blue sky darkened. Fluffy, rolling banks of clouds were left behind the soaring craft. Stars winked into sparkling life like distant diamonds atop the blackest of velvets.

. . .   *sixty-nine-and-a-seventy-and-a-seventy-one-and-a-seventy* . . .

The crushing hand abruptly released her. Replacing it was the weightlessness of null-gee. Air rushed in to fill Lizina's lungs, now free of the restraints of normal gravity raised to the sixth power. She swallowed hard.

The thunder of thrusting rockets faded to a lingering buzz in her ears. She raised a shaky hand to push a stray strand of copper-hued hair from her forehead. She smiled.

Free! I made it! I'm free!

The smile broadened to a wide self-confident grin. She *was* free! After the months of abuse, fear, plotting, and dreaming! It seemed so easy! It had taken her only thirty-six hours standard to find a way offplanet.

The shuttle lazily rolled to its side.

Lizina leaned to the right. A small, round porthole presented her with a view of Mirjam. Her last, she hoped with all her being.

From here, above the mining world, the planet's reds, coppers, and occasional streaks of electric greens appeared deceptively magnificent. Mirjam was anything but magnificent.

Mirjam was an apartment of hell for those living on its surface. A desert world, the planet provided no natural haven for the men—and rare woman—who came to rob her of her precious copper. Mirjam offered only heat, sand, and wind.

Lizina's broad smile remained. She was free! Free of Mirjam and her life of bondage there.

She was on her way home. Home! Home to Panish. And the comforts of a rich widow that awaited her there.

Panish.

The word rolled through her mind with an alien feel. It sounded so distant; so estranged to her enslaved existence of the past months.

The months stretched like years in retrospect—in sheer endurance. In actuality, less than six standard months had passed since she had been kidnapped from the security and comfort of Panish. In those months she had lived two to five lifetimes.

Now it's time to go home.

She closed her eyes and leaned against the couch's headrest. Panish wasn't home anymore. It had never truly been home. Though in a not too distant past, it had appeared to be everything she had ever wanted.

Now she knew differently. Dorjan had shown her that.

For the majority of her twenty-eight years, Lizina had called Lanatia home. Captain Jonuta of Qalara had changed that.

(She lied to herself. Her own stupidity had brought the change.)

A would-be singer and sometime hust on Lanatia, Lizina had taken part in a less than successful assassination attempt on the infamous slaver. When Jonuta and his crew were through using her (and use her they did, in every orifice her body provided), she had been abandoned in Harmony on planet Panish with a dress, a few stells for room and board for a night, and the name Coppertop.*

In Harmony (not spiritually, mentally, or physically; that was the strange world's capital city) Coppertop had been forced to ply her talents in the galaxy's oldest profession. She had been a hust, a cake to slice, spreading for any man—or woman—with the right price.

Garold Harith, one of the wealthiest men onplanet, had entered Coppertop's life.

And made a respectable woman out of me. The eons-old phrase floated through Lizina's mind.

Garold bought her from the brothel where she was employed. He cleaned her up, gave her a job, and returned her self-respect. He also gave her something she had never known before—love. Then he gave her his name. Coppertop became Lizina Harith, wife of Garold Harith.

The marriage lasted six months. Garold Harith was killed in a freak industrial accident, something that should not have happened in a place where he should not have been. Lizina had mourned his death, for she had loved him as she had never loved before.

When the socially prescribed period of Panish mourning had passed, Lizina shed the black garments of a widow and went in search of a casual lover for a night. The selected man had been one Thax Wilanu.

The evening had not ended as she had planned. Instead, Lizina was drugged and sold in bondage to one Captain Kukis of Shankar. Thax and a taxi driver she knew only by the name Mikk had been responsible for the transaction.

Thax and Mikk. They were the top names on a mental list she kept. When she reached Panish, she

---

* Spaceways #1: *Of Alien Bondage.*

would see that the kindness they had shown her was repaid in like currency—with interest added.

Lizina also intended to reciprocate the hospitality tendered her by Kukis and his First Mate Degula on the spacer *Forerunner*. The two had shown a decided relish for inflicting pain both mental and physical before they sold her as a hust onboard that Reshan Ganesa's *Be Lively*.

Only a few days ago Lizina had completed her recovery from the tetrazombase programming of her personality—compliments of Kukis and Degula. With repeated small dosages of the will-robbing drug they had stolen everything Garold had given her. No, not money. They stole more. They transformed her into the perfect, ever-obedient, ever-willing slave.

Exactly the type of woman Ganesa needed for *Be Lively!*

Dorjan.

The name came now like a silent prayer to her mind. *Dorjan*. She would be with him again. No one would stop her.

No one!

Dorjan and his crew of motley misfits had rescued her from Ganesa. Had shown her their world within an asteroid. HOME, they called it. To her the colony was simply home. A real home, to which she would eventually return. The home in which she would give birth to the child she now carried. Dorjan's son.

She would still be within the security of HOME had it not been for Ganesa. The Reshi had searched the spaceways for her stolen property. Had found that property—Lizina Harith. Had reclaimed her.

And in the treacherous process the spacegoing madam had kidnapped Kefira.

Lizina had no inkling of what had happened to the Akil woman. She tried not to think of her fate. Lizina prayed to Booda that it had been—was—better than her own.

In revenge for Lizina's rebellion, Ganesa had sold her on Mirjam to a man named Sofian Mahir. Lizina was supposed to be the mine foreman's wife. Legally, she was.

Since Mirjam was a woman-poor planet, Mahir saw his purchased wife as a means for making a small fortune on the mining world. Lizina was forced to hust. On her back and on her knees, she survived.

Survived. Lived.

She thought of that, of the future, rather than to ponder the endless line of miners Mahir had brought to share his wife's bed. For a price. His price.

Lizina glanced down at Mirjam. She had no regrets at leaving the planet. None at all . . . *No, wait.*

One regret, perhaps, she admitted to herself.

His name was Chane. The young miner had shown her kindness and love when all the others who had come to her bed had wanted only a cake to slice.

Chane was no longer on Mirjam. He had left the mining world a day before she gathered the courage to make her own escape.

She smiled again. Escape had not come without the sweetness of revenge. When she had last seen Mahir, the swine was dancing beneath the sonic beam of that universal weapon of Galactics, a stopper. Lizina had personally arranged that with relish, wedging the gun between two big stones so that it would continue to function until its power-pack was depleted.

The stopper was the modified version carried by those who traveled the spaceways beyond the Carnadyne Void. It had the usual three settings. *One* merely jangled the nerves to make its victim dance uncontrollably. Setting *Two* brought instantaneous unconsciousness.

Three killed and incinerated the victim's body to a pile of gray ash, if left on long enough. Oh-so-tidy and oh-so-efficient, that rod-shaped little single-handed weapon!

Lizina had left Mahir dancing within a beam generated by the stopper's first setting (with him naked and in the middle of a Mirjam desert). While the sonic beam wouldn't kill, sustained exposure would turn the man's brain to curd.*

And there *was* at least three days-standard worth of beam in the pistol's power-pack.

Did Mahir still live? Lizina hoped so. Death would be too easy for him. Too simple a repayment for what he had done to her.

The shuttle rolled again. Mirjam was replaced by a field of stars outside the porthole.

"There's *Lanna's Run*." The co-pilot's head turned back toward the lone passenger. He pointed to three mated metallic spheres directly in front of the ship's nose.

"It doesn't look like much from here. But it's a good, sturdy ship," he assured her. "Captain Bururia is as good as they come. She's been making the run between here and the Barbro Transfer Station since Mirjam was first opened."

Lizina nodded pleasantly. She didn't give a damn what *Lanna's Run* looked like. All it had to do was get her to Barbro. From there, she would find a way to Panish. If she had to pay every stell she carried for passage, she would. If she had to share the bed and embraces of a lusty spacer en route to the planet, she would.

The vibration of maneuvering rockets ran through the shuttle. Gently it swung into a parallel course with the larger ship.

"Soon as we're alongside, we'll run an S-corridor to *Lanna's Run*." The co-pilot turned to Lizina again.

---

* Spaceways #5: *Master of Misfit*.

"That'll be easier than suiting up and floating to the airlock."

She nodded her thanks. Actually, she would have preferred the latter. She had never donned a spacesuit and stepped outside the hull of a spacer, and she had learned to cope with new experiences. Some were even fun.

Lizina remained silent. There was no need to stamp on the fellow's display of courtesy. Besides, before she completed what she intended to do, space would no longer be an alien environment.

Lizina edged to the front of her couch. She peered at the growing form of the ship that would transport her to the Barbro Transfer Station. Excitement tingled through her.

Lizina, you've done it. You're on your way home. On your way HOME!

Captain Bururia was long, tall and stringy. Her hair was a cup of jet close-cropped to her skull. Practical rather than attractive. She was also one hundred and twenty per cent business.

"We don't see many passengers onboard *Lanna's Run*." The red-jumpsuited woman led Lizina down a cylindrical tunnel. "Two on one jaunt is a record."

Captain Bururia was also redundant. Lizina had met the spacefarer yesterday, and she had explained all this then. Lizina did not mind the fact that she would have to share *Lanna's Run*'s one and only passenger cabin with another person. That the passenger was male didn't matter either. Bururia had assured her the room's two beds were equipped with privacy screens.

If the screen were not enough to waylay any unwarranted attention from her roommate, Lizina had her stopper. Her right hand brushed the handle of the cylindrical gun strapped to her waist. Until her escape from

Mahir she had never worn a weapon. Now she would not be caught without one.

At a four-way tunnel junction, Bururia turned right and halted before a door painted a dull institutional green. She thumbed the hatch open and motioned Lizina inside before her. Her expression was her idea of pleasant.

The room was a cramped four meters by four meters, with two wall-attached beds on each side. A yellow surlock-expanbag lay on the bed to the right. Lizina tossed her small hand-held bag atop the one on the left.

"Sonic shower-sitter combo." Bururia pointed to a door at the rear of the room. "Meals are served in a common galley on Level Two three times a day. Chow-call's one long buzzer burst followed by three short. We've got a cybercook, but it was programmed by the best *human* chef on Hawking." She managed a smile.

Lizina nodded. She noted the privacy screen's button-controls on the side of her bed. Near the pillow, for easy access.

"My fellow passenger?"

"He agreed to help with the cargo to cut his fare." Bururia gave the room a once-over and nodded. "Cargo detail should be through in a half hour. Another thirty minutes and we hit the Tachyon Trail."

"Time enough for a shower before we're outbound then?"

"Time enough." Bururia redshifted through the hatch, closing it behind her.

Lizina ran a finger down the seamless front of the dull tan jumpsuit that was standard attire on Mirjam—for man or woman. Molecular bonding opened. She tossed her shoulders and let the suit drift about her ankles, then kicked it atop her bed. It didn't look any prettier off, but she did.

A shower now would avoid an awkward situation later when her male roommate was present. Conscious-ly, she gave her body cursory inspection. A habit retained from the days when her physical attributes were her only assets, and thus marketable.

Twenty-eight years old (plus a few months), she appeared a not-so innocent twenty-one. She stood a hundred sixty-eight sems and weighed a constant fifty-four kilos.

A bit fleshy for those with a taste for tall, stringy women such as Captain Bururia, she admitted. But for those with an eye for alluring curves rather than jutting bones, there was no denying the sensual voluptuousness of her consummately feminine form.

She had never given her breasts more than an "adequate" rating. Others would have been quick to disagree. Golden tan like the rest of her, they were firm and uptilted.

Most importantly to her, every sem of her body was *hers*. Naturally hers. A rarity in the Galactic worlds where cosmetic surgery and bioengineering were generally available to nearly everyone.

Even the metallic-coppery gleam of her hair was natural—right down to each and every root. Only her irises had been enhanced. Subcutane-treated to achieve a deep emerald hue.

Lizina ran a hand over the taut flatness of her belly. It would be months before the child she carried began to show. She thanked Emalia Daktari for that. HOME's physician had given her an injection that inhibited gestation. Her pregnancy would take eighteen months rather than the usual nine.

More than enough time to return HOME. The thought warmed her as she stepped toward the sonic shower. Her son—Dorjan's son—would be born on a world that traveled between the stars.

Lizina napped through the instant of mental and physical disorientation that accompanied *Lanna's Run*'s transition into a stream of coalesced tachyons. She had no complaints at having missed it.

It was the hiss of the room's opening door that woke her. She blinked leadened eyelids twice. . . . then sat up straight, eyes saucer-wide in disbelief.

"Chane!"

"Lizina?" The young man's expression contained the same incomprehension as hers. "How did . . . Lizina!"

He was on the bed beside her, hugging her joyously, kissing her lips and cheeks. She returned the enthusiastic greeting measure for measure.

Only four days ago she had sent this boy from her bedroom. (She thought of him as a boy because of the seven years separating their ages, though Chane had proven himself a man time and again in her bed.) They had said their teary-eyed goodbyes. She had never expected to see him again.

"Mahir? How did you get away from that son-of-a-vug?" Chane asked after the flurry of hugs and kisses subsided.

As Lizina began her explanation, a long buzzer sounded from a grille in the cabin's ceiling. It was followed by three short bursts. Chow-call.

Arm in arm, the young man and older woman found the way to Level Two and the galley. With Chane's demand for every minute detail of her flight from the mining town Ore City, Lizina's recount of her escape from Mahir more than adequately consumed the dinner conversation. It continued to occupy their attention during the stroll back to their cabin.

"If Mahir's stopper was equipped with one of those new high duration power-packs, he will be dancing for a week." Chane laughed in shared relish of Mahir's fate.

His youthful face abruptly went sober as the door hissed closed behind them. He turned to Lizina. His hands firmly gripped her shoulders.

"When you wouldn't run away with me . . . I didn't think you'd ever have the courage to make a break, Lizina."

"Neither did I. Not then."

That last day in Ore City, Chane had offered to help her escape from her husband/procurer. Lizina had refused. Mahir had killed a former "wife" and lover when they tried to run from him. She had not wanted Chane—or herself—to suffer a similar fate.

"Lizina, I never expected to see you again. To find you here with me is more than I ever hoped for." His voice was low and somber. "What I said in Ore City was real. I meant it. I love you, Lizina."

His hands tightened, drawing her to him. Hungrily, but with the gentleness she had always appreciated, his mouth covered hers. She offered no protest. The kiss seemed natural and right. After all, this was *Chane*.

And he did love her.

(In truth Lizina suspected that his love was a classical case of younger man and older woman. An infatuation that stemmed from the fact that she had been the only woman in Ore City—the only available woman.)

In her own way, she loved this boy/man. She had been no more than a piece of meat to all those Mahir had brought to her bed. A cake to slice. A hust with whom, in whom to relieve biological needs.

Chane had been different. He had cared, had given her love and friendship. In his innocence, he had wanted to protect her from Mahir. He would have killed himself trying to do so, if she had allowed him.

Chane's right hand released her shoulder. Fingertips glided to the neck of her jumpsuit. Molecular binding opened easily. Inward, beneath the coarse fabric, his hand slid. Warm palm cupped pliant breast.

"No!"

Lizina pushed from him. Anger twinged her denial.

Chane's forehead furrowed with uncertainty. "But

. . . Lizina . . .'' He stammered in confusion, his face stricken.

"This isn't Ore City! Chane, I'm not Mahir's property now.'' Lizina took a deep breath to steady herself, to quiet the anger. When she spoke again, it was with unmistakable determination.

"I *will not* be used again. *Never!* If a man comes to my bed, it will because *I* want him there. I'm not a hust. I won't be used like one. Never again.''

"Lizina, I . . .'' Chane still stammered, bewildered by the unexpected rejection. "Oh, *Lizina!*''

Lizina stared at him. "It won't be any other way, Chane. Do you understand that?''

He nodded slowly. Like a cowering puppy, he turned and sank to the edge of his bed. His gaze was downturned to the floor.

Lizina studied him while she sat on her own bed. *Damn it!*

She felt guilt. Chane and she had been lovers. Lovers of circumstance, she admitted, but lovers just the same. Perhaps she had been too sharp with him. The kiss, the caress of her breast were things he had done hundreds of times before.

No. With resolution, she assured herself. She was free of everything she had been on Mirjam. *From now on, I choose who shares my bed.* That was the way it had to be; that was the way it *would* be.

"Chane, there is something we need to talk about.''

He looked up. The hurt in his eyes tore at her heart. She did her damnedest to ignore them. She was her own woman now. And she intended to remain that way.

"There are some things I've never told you about Lizina Harith,'' she said, to begin a thumbnail history of her life on Panish.

Chane's eyes widened with each word she spoke. She saw doubt on his face. But beneath that was definite interest. She told him of Thax, Mikk, Kukis, Degula, and Ganesa. Then of Dorjan and HOME—without, carefully, mentioning any of them by name. She would have died before betraying either of those trusts.

"What I am saying is that I need somebody to help me. Someone I can trust." She paused, her eyes meeting his and holding them in green bonds. "There's only one person I know who fills that bill. You."

Chane said nothing. Traces of a hurt puppy remained in his expression.

"I know you want to get back to your home on Jasbir," Lizina continued to plead her case. "But I promise you that if you'll stay with me, help me, I'll make it well worth your while."

"I don't know. You've got to admit that from where I stand it all sounds pretty fantastic." Chane shrugged.

"I've lived through it. And it seems fantastic to me." Lizina smiled sadly. Chane had no reason to believe her. "All I can say is that everything I've told you is true."

He shrugged again. "I'll have to think about it."

"You've got until we reach the Barbro Transfer Station to make a decision. From there, *I* find passage to Panish."

"Let me sleep on it, Lizina."

She nodded. "A good idea. It's been a long day, and I could use a week or three of sleep."

Lizina swung her legs onto the bed while Chane rose and buttoned the overhead lights. The light dimmed to a soft glow, but did not go off.

A precaution for green spacefarers who might lose their way in the dark? Lizina wondered.

She toed off her shoes and kicked them to the floor. Starting to wiggle free of the jumpsuit, she paused. Chane still stood by the light control. He stared at her intently.

No need making it worse on him than it already is.

She felt along the side of the bed and found the privacy screen buttons. She pressed one.

An opaque gray field formed about the bed. Chane and his sad-pup's eyes were the last things Lizina saw as the screen went up. Rootless guilt (or was it?) suffused her again.

She tried to repress the feeling while she peeled away her jumpsuit and tossed it to the foot of the bed. Why should she feel guilty? Chane had no right to expect anything else from her! They weren't on Mirjam!

On Mirjam he had me . . .

Had me . . .

A surprising tingle raced through her body. What they had shared had been good. She smiled.

Damn good.

Chane was young in years. But he definitely understood what a woman—at least *this* woman—wanted from a man. And he knew how to provide it.

An image of hurt eyes, eyes so young, niggled at her mind.

She reached for the privacy screen controls.

No.

She jerked her hand away. She wouldn't give in to him. She was her own woman and intended to remain that way. Only those she chose would share her bed.

Her lip firmed, twitched . . .

Her smile returned.

Isn't the choice mine now? He hasn't tried to force me to do anything I don't want.

And at the moment, she wanted someone beside her, holding her, loving her. Someone who cared. She wanted it very much! *So . . . choose!*

She threw out a hand and tapped the privacy screen controls. The gray field dissolved. Across the room, Chane's head jerked around.

Unashamed of her nakedness, Lizina rolled to face

him. She smiled widely. "There's room enough for two over here."

He needed no further encouragement.

Shedding his clothes as he crossed the room, Chane came to her. The kisses, the caressing hands she had rejected such a short time before were hers once again. She reveled in them. She gave herself freely to them and the electric sensations they awoke in her body.

There was little sleep that night as *Lanna's Run* sliced across light-years laughing in the face of Einstein's proclamation. Neither Lizina nor Chane cared about the lack of sleep or the light-years they crossed.

3

Dorjan sat at *Misfit*'s control console. His hands tensed and relaxed. Three-sem unipolymer plasteel claws extended and retracted from his fingertips.

The action came unconsciously, a habit that lingered from a time when those claws had often saved his life in the arena of Harb.

Since his escape from slavery, Dorjan had not used the treacherously concealed claws against another person. Now he was prepared to use them (or any other weapon onboard) to save his ship and crew from the predator that hung in space fifty meters off *Misfit*'s starboard side.

Dorjan stared at the image relayed from the optical sensors attached to *Misfit*'s hull. An airlock slid open along *Lung T'ou*'s port side. The dark, featureless maw expelled three spacesuited figures.

Red Rover . . .

Dorjan toed open intraship comm. "Three of them are on their way. Repeat *three*, not four. Red, yellow, and glo-green suits. Red's armed with a plasma gun. Yellow and green have stoppers only."

"Affirmative," Songan's voice answered from the grille. "Lead yellow and green this way. Iniko, Hedeon, and I will take care of the rest!"

Dorjan killed the intraship link. He signaled Yuw to follow him to the airlock to receive their boarders. Unarmed, as SotKil demanded.

The three waiting within the drive chamber, however, weren't. Songan and crew carried two stoppers each They were also armored in spacesuits.

The fight awaiting yellow and green would hardly be fair. But then fairness didn't win fights. Brains did, with the aid of brawn. Songan had both. And he knew how to use them.

That left red and the fourth member of *Lung T'ou* to be dealt with, and without weapons.

Number four would have to wait until the first three were out of the way, leaving only red to contend with at once. Dorjan had no doubt that red was SotKil himself. He was betting his life that he was right.

The bastard's crazy!

Only a madman would carry a plasma gun onboard a ship. As with a laser, one misplaced shot could hole the hull. The results of that would . . .

Misfit's captain did not consider the possible results. The time for caution had passed.

Hands tensed and relaxed. Claws slid out and retracted.

Songbird and Edrek waited by the airlock. Unarmed, both of them. Neither Jarp nor man said anything; both stared hopelessly at their captain.

"Stand to the left. Near the hatch." Dorjan motioned to his three companions. "If SotKil intends to shoot first and ask questions later, you'll have a chance to get to your weapons."

The trio did as ordered while Dorjan stood directly before the inner door of the airlock. Sweat trickled from his armpits in wet rivulets.

A metallic *clang* came from beyond the double-plated hatch. The outer door was locked. From within the lock came the soft hiss of air's being pumped in to replace the vacuum of space. The lock's inner door slid back. The pirates had Red Rovered.

Plasma gun aimed directly at Dorjan's stomach, Redsuit

stepped into *Misfit*. Yellow and green followed, stoppers leveled before them.

"Captain Dasan." Redsuit nodded his helmeted head.

Though the round helm was opaqued to conceal the face within, the voice was SotKil's—the Hammer Fist.

Dorjan tilted his head in reply. His TPs narrowed for an instant to focus on the sem-wide ribbon cable that ran from the butt of the pirate's blaster to a power-pack strapped to the left thigh of his scarlet spacesuit.

"Captain, we can handle this two ways. The right way and the wrong way." SotKil motioned for green and yellow to cover Dorjan's three crewmembers.

"The right way—the least painful way—is simply direct us to what we want. When we've got that, we'll leave you in peace. With your DS disabled, of course."

SotKil paused, apparently studying Dorjan from behind the smoky faceplate of his helmet. "The wrong way is to make me search for the TZ. Should that be your choice, I'll begin the search by eliminating you. That should make your crew more cooperative. Understood?"

Dorjan frowned and counted to ten. A charade for the benefit of the pirate. To give in too easily, without some outward sign of consternation would have been as foolish as refusing the demand of the coolly arrogant slime.

Again Dorjan nodded. "I'll . . . send one of my men for the TZ. Yuw, go below and . . ."

SotKil laughed loudly. "Not so fast, Dasan! Your man needs some company. He might get lost along the way . . . or bring back more than the TZ."

Lung T'ou's captain again motioned to his fellow hijackers. Yuw glanced at Dorjan as though uncertain of what he was to do.

"Move it, you Outie sisterslicer!" Dorjan swiveled in mock rage. He waved Varn on. "Captain SotKil's no fool. If they want the weapons, show them where we stowed them!''

''Just the TZ, Outreacher,'' SotKil amended the order.

''Just the TZ, Varn,'' Dorjan said in a resigned voice.

With Varn in the lead, yellow and green ducked through the hatch to make their way to the nonexistent tetrazombase. Dorjan repressed a smile.

So far, so good. Now for the Hammer Fist and his plasma gun!

The barrel of that weapon thrust into the small of Dorjan's back.

''Over there with your crew, Dasan,'' SotKil ordered, with another nudge of the gun.

Dorjan complied, positioning himself two meters from Songbird. He turned back to stare at the red-spacesuited pirate. The thick barrel of the gun returned the stare.

If SotKil decided to squeeze the trigger now, the blast would cut *Misfit*'s captain in two and melt half the bulkhead behind him.

An inner bulkhead—not *Misfit*'s hull. The blast would not seriously harm the spacer. Which was exactly what Dorjan wanted. (Minus being seared into two equally dead portions.)

Hand loosely balled at his side, Dorjan extended plasteel claws. Now all there was to do was wait—and watch.

Dorjan narrowed his three-hundred-sixty-degree vision to encompass SotKil only. His attention focused on the gleaming red helmet. When the time came, there would be no warning, merely a startled jerk of that helmet (if that).

A split second of surprise and confusion in which to act—or die!

So Dorjan waited. Waited. And waited.

A slight tilt of the helmet.

Dorjan dropped and leaped forward, knowing that

cries of surprise echoed within SotKil's space helmet. Warning cries as yellow and green found themselves face to face with Songan, Iniko, and Hedeon.

SotKil's hand tightened about the plasma gun. Crackling blue fire erupted from the wide muzzle.

Stoppers were not designed for armored personnel. A man or woman enclosed in the protection of a spacesuit was just that. Even on its third setting, a stopper's sonic blast could not penetrate the metallex shield of a spacesuit.

It could, however, transform a spacesuit into a self-contained oven. Sustained exposure to a stopper's sonic beam would, in effect, *cook* the individual within the metallic shell.

Three stoppers did the job three times as fast.

And six stoppers (three each) were what yellow and green faced the moment they stepped into the room containing *Misfit*'s drive.

As pre-arranged, Varnalgeran Yuw dropped to the deck and rolled backwards. Between the would-be plunderers and through the hatchway rolled the overweight Outie, tumbling with astonishing speed. Outside, beyond the reach of stopper beams, he buttoned the hatch closed. The two pirates were sealed inside with his spacesuit-protected crewmates.

Inside, Songan and his two companions squeezed the stoppers they held in both hands. Yellow and green squeezed the firing grips of their weapons in return.

Two stoppers did not equal six. That fact apparently became clear to yellow in a matter of a very few heated seconds. Tossing his stopper aside, yellow launched himself at the blue-suited figure nearest him.

A mistake, that.

Songan wore the blue spacesuit. Even in the clumsy shell of metal, *Misfit*'s First Mate remained as deadly as when he had stood naked in the arena of Harb.

Dropping his stoppers, Songan pivoted to the left

before his attacker's head-on charge. As the yellow-suited pirate shot by, completely missing his intended victim, Songan's hands whipped out. He grasped the tether-line ring on yellow's shoulder and the utility belt about his waist.

Using yellow's own momentum, Songan swung the man head first into the nearest bulkhead. It was a maneuver that in a long-forgotten parlance had been called the bum's rush.

Yellow dropped to the floor and stayed there.

Songan whirled around. Green stood against the wall with both hands raised high above his head. Iniko and Hedeon had their four stoppers leveled at the pirate.

"Get them out of their suits and lock them in hold B-2."

Songan didn't wait for confirmation of his order but moved to the hatch and pounded on it three times. It opened. With Yuw, Songan rushed toward *Misfit's* airlock.

Heat seared along Dorjan's back. Only heat! The plasma bolt sizzled harmlessly over him.

It was SotKil's one and only shot. Dorjan's clawed hand closed around the ribbon cable that connected gun to power-pack. He yanked. The cable tore free of the pistol's butt, leaving it totally useless.

In the next instant, Dorjan hit the deck in a roll. He came to his feet, twisting to face the pirate captain.

"You're alone, SotKil. Gi . . ."

Dorjan didn't have the chance to complete his sentence. SotKil charged. His armored arms were open wide to ensnare the unprotected Harbian.

Dorjan stood his ground before the onrushing man. At the last instant, he ducked and leaped aside. With surprising alacrity, the pirate pivoted to face him once again . . . and charged again.

Dorjan ducked beneath the attack once more. An instant too slowly.

SotKil's armored fist slammed into Dorjan's shoulder. Off balance, *Misfit*'s captain lost his footing. He fell, sliding across the metal floor head-on into an unyielding wall of equally hard metal.

Through the dazing pain, he saw a gleaming red foot descending toward his head.

The foot never reached him. Songan, still in his blue spacesuit, was there. Hands on SotKil's shoulders, the First Mate yanked backwards.

The pirate captain hit the deck hard. He lay there struggling to right himself. The metal floor offered no hold for the metalloid spacesuit. Like a turtle on its back, the Hammer Fist rolled from side to side, almost helpless.

Dorjan pushed to his feet. He ran a hand over short-cropped white hair. An egg-sized bump swelled on the back of his head, throbbing painfully. The reminder of his encounter with SotKil would be with him for days.

"Get him to his feet and strip him of the suit. Then toss him in with the others in B-2," Songan ordered as he walked to his captain.

Songan bent to retrieve a dark brown wig from the floor and handed it to Dorjan. The hair of Captain Dasan, jarred from Dorjan's head during the fight.

"We've still got another of SotKil's crew to deal with." Dorjan watched his friend twist the blue helmet and pull upward. A grinning face eerie with multi-colored tattoos was unveiled.

Songan shrugged. "Perhaps our Captain SotKil might be convinced to persuade his last crewmate to surrender without a fight?"

Dorjan glanced to his right as Songan and Edrek pulled the pirate captain to his feet. "I wouldn't . . ."

SotKil threw his arms back. Unable to maintain a grip on the snug-fitting suit, Songbird and Edrek were shaken free with a minimum of effort. SotKil raced toward the still open airlock.

"Son-of-a-vug!"

Dorjan pushed pass his Mate. The Saipese captain couldn't be allowed to escape. If he reached the well-armed *Lung T'ou* . . .

Dorjan leaped, arms wide to encircle the escaping man's legs. He caught one . . . in a less than firm grip.

SotKil kicked outward. Dorjan clung to the red suit, fingers slipping. He wouldn't be able to hold. Bio-engineered muscles flexed in Dorjan's right forefinger. A softly humming vibe-knife unsheathed from the end of a fingertip.

Dorjan jabbed inward and jerked to the right as SotKil kicked out again. There was an instant of resistance, then the vibrating blade sliced into the red spacesuit.

In the next instant, the Saipese pirate was free. He darted into the airlock, slamming a palm against a pressure plate just inside. The hatch slid closed.

The last thing Dorjan saw was a two-sem slice in the ankle of SotKil's suit.

The hiss of air being sucked from the airlock came from behind the double-plated hatch . . . and the air that was sucked from the tiny slit in the ankle of a spacesuit, leaving only vacuum for its occupant to breathe.

Dorjan stood.

The outer door to the lock never opened. Captain SotKil of *Lung T'ou* was dead.

"Get the bastard's carcass out of there!" Dorjan's order came as a sharp bark.

For the first time in over ten years he had killed. That the man was a murderous pirate who had deserved to die didn't make it any easier. Killing, to Dorjan of Harb, was killing.

"Songan, get the drive up. Now!" Dorjan turned to Yuw. "Come with me. We've one more of SotKil's men to deal with!"

SotKil's remaining crew member wasn't a man. She was a very green spacefarer who stammered over the intership comm when Dorjan detailed what had happened to her captain and other crewmates.

For a pulse-racing moment, Dorjan thought she might try something stupid despite the fact that *Misfit*'s DS was training on *Lung T'ou*. With only fifty meters separating the ships, even a scared and green hand could do a lot to damage before she could be stopped.

She didn't.

Instead she did as ordered. Abandoned *Lung T'ou*'s controls, suited up, and docilely crossed to *Misfit* where Songbird and Edrek desposited her in hold B-2 with her two companions.

Dorjan swiveled from the console to stare at his computrician. A weak smile uplifted the corners of his mouth as though to say—*we did it, but I'll be damned if I know how!*

"What I need is a drink. A tall, cold drink!"

"There's Starflare still onboard," Yuw said, suggesting the renowned beer from the planet Thebanis.

"Stronger, Varn. *Much* stronger!"

The Outie grinned and pushed from his seat. "On Outreach we have a drink called Theba's Heaven. Guaranteed to make you a true believer, Captain. If you're willing to wait while I do some concocting?"

Dorjan waved Varn off. The drink sounded as though it would have the same effects as TZ. "Make it a Starflare. No, make it two!"

Arms spread wide like two thick pillars, Songan leaned on the console and studied *Lung T'ou* in a three-dimensional holographic display. The ship was still. All systems down and abandoned.

"It would be a damn' waste to leave it adrift." *Misfit*'s First Mate pushed from the con and turned to his captain.

Dorjan nodded. "I've been thinking the same thing. We could always do some revamping and sell it for a handy profit on any inner planet."

"Then there's the problem of our three unwanted guests in B-2." Songan sank into the Mate's chair beside his friend. His gaze returned to the monitor and *Lung T'ou*.

"If we could get SotKil's crew and the ship to HOME, we could solve both problems."

"We're only one jump from Mirjam. HOME's a long way in the wrong direction." Songan lifted a skweez-bulb of Starflare and emptied a quarter of the contents in one gulp. "Though Emalia Daktari could handle our problem with the three in B-2."

Partial brainwipes were the standard procedure for those freed slaves brought to HOME who could not adjust to life in the asteroid colony. HOME's physician erased any knowledge of the colony and its location from their minds, then the slaves were returned (free) to the planet of their choice.

The same technique could be used on *Misfit*'s three captive pirates. Dorjan smiled. Memory erasures of Captain Dasan and *Nobigthing* would protect The Shadow Walker. Of course, all knowledge of SotKil and their activities under the Saipese's command would have to go, too.

All in all, they might be better off than they were with SotKil.

The master of *Misfit* knew they would better off than had they been captured by some other spacer. Usual procedure along the spaceways would have been to dump them into space—without benefit of a spacesuit. (And someone such as that flainer Jonuta might have *sold* them!)

"What about Iniko and Hedeon?" Dorjan glanced at his fellow Harbian. "Think they could handle *Lung T'ou* by themselves?"

Songan sat quietly a moment, then nodded. "It would be better if there was someone else with them. But . . ."

"But, I don't want to cut *Misfit*'s crew any more than I have to," Dorjan finished his Mate's sentence with a firmness that confirmed he would not consider three men for the unexpected flight.

"In that case, Iniko and Hedeon are quite capable of handling *Lung T'ou* alone," Songan acquiesced with a shrug.

"Good. Let's get them up here and break the news. The sooner they're on the way back to HOME, the sooner we get to Mirjam."

And Lizina, Dorjan thought as he opened intraship comm to summon the two men to the con-cabin.

4

On the outer edge of the Carnadyne Void, far from the star-crowded area toward the galaxy's center, beyond Skylla and Karybdis, hung the Barbro Transfer Station.

Like the space stations that orbited Galactic-inhabited planets, Barbro was torus-shaped, a spinning wheel that generated centrifugal force and the illusion of point-eight normal gravity. In the case of Barbro, though, there were twelve wheels. Each was three times larger than a planetary space station. All were connected by a cylindrical hub running through the center of each.

It was here the spacers came: the ships from the Farther Reaches with holds crammed and tether lines of attached cargo untidily astream behind them. Barbro also attracted the *big* ships, vessels kloms in length. These gargantuans served the Rim Worlds, planets perched on the very edges of the galaxy where the spiral arm trailed off into the void.

Barbro accepted cargo from each and stored it until the arrival of the spaceship, big or small, slated for the merchandise. Ten of Barbro's wheels were designated as warehouses.

Barbro thrived on docking and storage fees.

Level Two, Barbro's second wheel was devoted solely to servicing the spacers. Providing repairs, modifications, and equipment updating. It was a lucrative trade in itself.

The uppermost wheel—Hometown—housed the ten

thousand men and women needed to maintain and operate the transfer station. Seventy per cent of the torus was relegated to living quarters for those ten thousand. Ten per cent officed Operation Control. The remaining twenty per cent was a compacted city of offices representing various freight lines and commercial entrepreneurs, shops and stores displaying items from throughout the galaxy (legal and illegal), and hotels. Mnemonic adverts chatted at the spacefarers who came to Barbro.

It was here, along a wide avenue lined with flashing signs and brightly lit storefronts, that Lizina wandered. She idly killed time in an eons-old pastime while she awaited Chane's return.

Lizina was window shopping.

Time and again, she browsed the exotic selection of dresses and gowns, tunics and tights (all duty free), displayed in the various shops. Now and again her head would turn while she studied the equally exotic (and often erotic) attire worn by passersby.

Dressed in her dull tan Mirjam jumpsuit, Lizina felt like an alien who had been inexplicably transported into an awesome world of unknown wonders. The colors, the eclectic blending of styles from the galaxy-spanning worlds brought a rush of tingling excitement—of anticipation. Something she had thought Mirjam had killed in her.

She hugged her single flight bag to her chest. A solid bulge pressed from beneath the fabric. A roll of stells; the remainder of Sofian Mahir's depleted credaccount. Money she had *earned,* and money she had thoughtfully taken before fleeing the mining world.

Her covetous gaze returned to a quietly decorated window that had repeatedly drawn her attention during her window browsing. Two subtly shifting cybermannikins stood behind an immaculately clean plate of duraglas. They wore exquisite gowns of rich forest green and midnight black.

Of the two, the reelsilk black was definitely the more alluring. The neckline V'd below the mannikin's plaskin navel. The floor-length skirt was slit up the right side to a point at which thigh became more than thigh.

Green *did* highlight the copper sheen of her hair . . .

Again, Lizina squeezed the flight bag to feel the security of the stells. Her skin could almost taste the luxury of reelsilk against it. *Either one of them would be nice. Make me feel like a woman again.*.

"Lizina!" Chane called to her. "Lizina!"

She turned full circle before locating him. He trotted toward her through the crowd of spacefarers within their Hometown. Chane's face was split from ear to ear with an enthusiastic grin.

"I've got us passage to Panish," he managed to sputter between gulps of air. "With a Captain Pentama-homet Ramzi. His ship's on Level Nine. We're sched-uled for departure in an hour. Ramzi said be onboard in thirty minutes or he'd leave without us! Moosejaw, they call him."

"Panish! Chane, you're a miracle worker!" Lizina hugged his neck and kissed his cheek. Loudly and wetly.

"I won't argue that." He beamed, almost glowing from her praise. "But we really have to get down to Level Nine. This Ramzi is an old bastard. Set in his ways, and not about to change them for anyone. If we're not on *India Spring* by his deadline, he *will* leave without us."

"Passage?" Lizina glanced back at the gowns. "How much for each of us?"

"Three kilostells."

Lizina swallowed at the price. "Three thousand—*each*?"

Chane nodded hesitantly. "You said find us direct passage. There's *Starduster* and *Shosnic*, but both are planet hopping. It'll be months before their circuits bring them to Panish. But if you want, I'll book passage on one of them. It'll be cheaper."

He paused and took a breath. "Or I could loan you what I have. If you're short."

Lizina shook her head with determination. "You're working for me now. And I said I'd foot the expenses."

She didn't look back to the store window. Passage with this Captain Ramzi would leave her just enough for taxi fare once she reached Panish. She had traveled this far in a jumpsuit. She could postpone a shopspree until she was onplanet—on Panish!

Then, she promised herself, *Chane and I go wild for a day. I deserve it!*

"Thirty minutes?" Lizina offered her new employee an arm. "We'd better go and meet this Captain Moosehead, or whatever his name is."

Chane took the proffered arm and led her toward Hometown's hub and its elevators that dropped to the lower levels. If the young man felt any embarrassment escorting such a shabbily attired woman, Lizina could not discern it from his broad grin.

She smiled. Damn, but she was glad he had decided to come with her. She needed someone, if only for moral support.

Their mutually satisfying romps in bed undoubtably had weighed the scales in her favor when Chane made that decision, she realized. She felt a bit guilty about it. Not guilty enough to stop, but enough to feel a few pangs of conscience.

"There's something else," Chane said abruptly, looking down at her.

"About Ramzi?"

"About Ganesa."

Lizina stopped and stared at her companion.

"Ganesa?"

"All of Barbro is buzzing with it. She went Forty Per Cent City. It happened right here four days ago."

It took a moment for Lizina to recall what going City meant. When she did, a hollow sensation tautened her stomach.

"Did she survive?"

Chane's head moved from side to side. "At least not as far as anyone's been able to determine."

"Damn!"

Anger replaced the hollowness. She had been cheated! Ganesa had been marked. Marked for her!

"What happened? Do you know any details?"

"No one's sure. Apparently *Be Lively* was being pursued by another spacer. A ship named *Nobigthing*. Captained by a Drisen or Disan. Something like that."

"Nobigthing." Lizina let the name roll from her lips. She was afraid she had heard wrong. Afraid to believe it was true. "Captain Dasan."

"That's his name. Dasan!" Chane stared at her, brow furrowing. "Do you know him?"

Lizina nodded and smiled. "Very well."

Very well, indeed!

Warmth spread joyously through her body. She tugged Chane toward the elevators.

Dasan was *Dorjan*! She was certain of that. She had heard him mention the name as one of The Demon Cat's endless disguises.

Which meant she hadn't been cheated. Only that Dorjan had found Ganesa and her ship first.

Lizina's smile widened to a pleased grin. Dorjan was looking for her! Even avenging her! Had he learned of Mirjam? Would it matter?

She shoved the uncertainty from her mind.

It wouldn't matter. For other men, riddled with masculine insecurities, the fact that their women had been forced to hust would totally crush their fragile egos. But not for Dorjan.

Not for Dorjan!

Tears of joy welled in her eyes and their sting was welcome. At the same time, she wore a foolish smile.

And he's searching for me.

Sooner or later, Dorjan and *Misfit* would come to Panish. He knew of her life there. Panish was the only logical choice for his search.

She pulled Chane along at a faster pace.

And I'll be there waiting for him!

5

Captain Nnamdi of the spacer *Long Hauler* entered the Mine Shaft Bar and Recreational Lounge. His eyes narrowed, though they did not see. He peered into the dimly lit, smoke-clouded room via a series of telepresences implanted about his neck like a string of dark pearls.

The TPs, boosted to infrared, saw the dark room as if it were inundated by the harsh, unrelenting Mirjam sun outside. Nnamdi/Dorjan of Harb shifted the optics back to normal human range. The Mine Shaft looked better that way.

Square-built from rough synthestone blocks with a root of unipolymer plasteel, the Mine Shaft was no more than a twenty-five by twenty-five-meter box. Tables (a mismatch of round and square) were scattered about the bar's single room with no thought for symmetry or design. A lone cyberbartender wheeled among the ten occupied tables.

Dorjan repressed the urge to grimace. The occupants of those tables appeared as rough and unpolished as the bar. Miners all.

The Mine Shaft offered little to recommend it as a meeting place. Except that it was one of two such establishments in Windbreak, capital city of the planet Mirjam. (The title of capital came by default. Windbreak, population twenty-five thousand, was twice as large as the mining planet's other ten colonies.) The

Mine Shaft was also across a dusty avenue from Windbreak's—and Mirjam's—solitary shuttleport (a single trinitite runway with a squatty building set in the south side).

Dorjan moved into the dimness and smoke. He selected a seat at a vacant table and ordered a beer from the cyberbartender. No Starflare, only a local brew that was several months too green. It bit from palate to stomach.

Half a beer later, Songan entered (tattooed skin subcutaned to an ebony black that equalled Captain Nnamdi's hue). Waving for the cyberbartender, *Misfit*'s First Mate dragged a chair beside Dorjan.

"You'll regret it," Dorjan said as his friend paid the automaton for a beer.

"Mirjam itself is a regrettable experience." Songan inhaled half the drink in two gulps. His face wrinkled in disgust. "Recycled piss!"

"I'm not certain about the recycling." Dorjan smiled and gingerly took another sip from his beer. The taste had not improved. He shoved the glass to the center of the table.

"Find anything else?" Songan edged his beer over beside Dorjan's.

Misfit's captain shook his head. "Nothing."

Before jam-cramming *Be Lively* into subspace with captain and crew, Dorjan had *persuaded* Ganesa to reveal where she sold Lizina. And to whom. In two days onplanet, he had learned little more.

Sofian Mahir, who had purchased Lizina, had been discovered wandering naked in the desert between Windbreak and the mining town Ore City. The man was a blubbering idiot, unable to do much more than sit and stare at a wall. Local physicians were uncertain of the source of his cottage-cheesed brains. The prognosis for recovery was nil.

Dorjan was helpless not to like that.

Coinciding with Mahir's mental deterioration was the disappearance of his wife . . . a woman known only as Coppertop in Ore City. A woman the mine foreman had married, then whored to his fellow miners.

Dorjan had no doubt that Mahir's wife was the same Coppertop he had once stolen from Ganesa's Traveling Bakery Shoppe, as *Be Lively* had been nicknamed by spacefarers. One Lizina Harith. His Lizina.

But where she had vanished remained unanswered.

"Have you ever noticed anything strange about your Outie computrician?"

Dorjan frowned at the odd question, then noticed Varnalgeran Yuw standing at the bar's entrance. The overweight man grinned when he sighted his companions. Gods, that shirt! The man had the taste of a Thebanian cess-rooter!

Dorjan chuckled. "Plenty. What have you just noticed?"

"Varn doesn't sweat." Songan studied the approaching Outie. "It must be forty-two* outside. I'm dripping sweat. You're dripping sweat. This whole damn world is sweating. And Varn looks like he just stepped from air-conned luxury. Not even a moist glisten on his forehead."

Songan was not exaggerating, although Dorjan couldn't see the man's forehead. It was hidden by the wide brim of the Wayne he wore—constantly wore.

The gaudy flowered shirt (complete with simulated mother-of-pearl buttons and embroidered arrows at the pockets) and faded denim pants (cuffs half-tucked into the tops of reptile skin-imitating, sharp-toed, equhyde boots) that Yuw wore hinted at no trace of sweat. Nor dust. Everything and everyone on Mirjam was dusty. Anyone, that is, who had been onplanet for more than two minutes.

---

* Celcius; about 106°, Old Style.

"Damn! It's a flainin' blast furnace out there!" Yuw pulled another chair to the table and plopped down. He looked at the abandoned beers and his face was an open question.

Both captain and Mate nodded.

Yuw lifted one and drained it. Eyebrows mobile over eyes alight, he chased it with the other. He smacked his lips with relish and grinned.

"Feel a bit better now." He called to the cyber-bartender for another beer.

"Our Outie friend also has a decided taste for grat piss." Songan winked at Dorjan.

"Recycled or otherwise." Dorjan laughed at the mock pained expression that transformed Varn's face into the image of a loose-skinned Harbian hunting hound.

"I assume you two uncultured escapists from galactic justice have taken it upon yourselves to compare the planet Outreach with the lesser worlds," Yuw said—in one uninterrupted breath—then punctuated the reprimand with a raised eyebrow that was just discernible in the shadow of his wide-rimmed hat.

"Never a world—just one Outie we all know and love." Songan replied with another wink.

"Hurumph!" Yuw snorted in continued mock indignation. "I've been out in that cruel Mirjam sun working my zork off while you two relax in this oasis—and all I get is insults. Serve you right were I to keep my lips sealed."

"You learned something?" Dorjan's head jerked up.

"Of course, I did, Captain." Yuw paused, dramatically letting the suspense mount. "I'm an Outie, aren't I?"

"You'll be an Outie minus his hide, if you don't share everything you've found out in about three seconds!"

Varn winked at his captain. "First, Lizina was officially and legally wed to Sofian Mahir. She also divorced him the day after she disappeared from Ore City. Also nice and legal. She did it right here in Windbreak. I've seen the court proceedings. Process, actually. Mirjam, despite its feminine name, is woman-hungry. If a woman wants to free herself of a man, all she has to do is file one document.''

Dorjan didn't question how Varn had uncovered this. The Outie protected his sources and methods of obtaining the impossible. But when it came to unraveling the red tape of the bureaucracy (and occasionally thoroughly snarling that red tape if need be) not even Songan could outmatch Yuw.

"Day after her divorce, Lizina booked passage on a spacer bound for the Barbro Transfer Station.'' Varn paused for a sip from his ordered beer. "She wanted passage to Panish. None of the spacers working Mirjam goes farther than Barbro.''

"Barbro!'' The name came like a curse from Dorjan's lips.

Six days ago—less than a week standard—*Misfit* had been docked at Barbro. The possibility—probability—that Lizina's spacer and *Misfit* had crossed paths as streams of tachyons moving in opposite directions was infuriating. Frustrating.

So damned close! Yet lightyears away!

"Panish,'' Songan repeated, his eyes shifting to Dorjan, "is a long way from Mirjam . . . and Ginneh.''

Panish seemed half the galaxy away. Dorjan slammed a fist atop the table. He cursed, using the profanity of three languages, including Jarp.

Panish, and Lizina, lay within the Farther Reaches. In the opposite direction lay Ginneh, and Kefira. Only Ginneh was two short hops from Mirjam.

"She's safe, Dorjan.'' Songan squeezed his friend's shoulder. "That's more than we knew when we came here. And we know we can find her on Panish.''

Dorjan nodded. There was no real choice between

Panish and Ginneh. First Ginneh and Kefira. Then Panish and Lizina. Logistics and nothing else governed the decision.

Lizina is safe. And Kefira?

All Dorjan knew of the alien woman was that Ganesa had sold her to a man named Mensah Nav, chief administrator of cyprium mining interests on the planet.

"I think it might be wise if we were carrying cargo," Songan suggested, glancing at Yuw. "Ginneh's off the usual routes. It wouldn't look right to show up there with empty holds."

"I'll handle it." Dorjan shoved from the table. "With luck we'll be off this Booda-forsaken planet by nightfall."

"With luck," Songan repeated as he and Yuw followed their captain out into the merciless Mirjam sun.

The Outie glanced longingly back at the big blinking BEER HERE sign.

6

Lizina impatiently shifted from one foot to the other while Panish Customs ran her small bag (contents: one spare jumpsuit) through a series of scan-probes. Four in all.

It would have been far faster had the gray-uniformed officers simply opened the go-bag, dumped the contents on the ground, and dredged through it by hand.

Instead it crept at a snail's pace along a cyberbelt to pass through the four sensor stations. All were manned by men who appeared more interested in the standings of Harmony's MercuryBall team than earning the tax stells they sucked from governmental teat on a weekly basis.

After an eternity, the bag trundled from the rectangular mouth of the final probe. Lizina grabbed its handle with one hand and Chane with the other.

"Now, you'll see that you made the right choice in sticking with me!" She grinned back at him while she wove through the stream of people moving through the shuttleport's terminal.

"I already know I made the right choice!" Chane laughed when she tugged eagerly on his arm. She was hastening him toward the glass doors at the front of the building.

Outside, Lizina sucked in a deep breath. She grinned widely, emerald eyes agleam.

"Air, Chane! *Panish* air! Taste it! No dust! No sand!

And feel the temperature! It's summer here, and it's so wonderfully cool!''

Again her companion laughed. "*Panish*—Booda's heavenly gift to humankind!''

"No sarcasm! Right now Panish seems like every concept of heaven neatly packaged in one planet.'' Her broad smile was undiminished by his comment.

Nothing could lessen the excitement that coursed through her. The instant the shuttle had lifted from Mirjam, she had known she was finally free.

Now, she realized it. Every cell in her body sang that freedom. She was Lizina Harith again. Completely, totally! Coppertop the hust, the slave, was gone, buried in the past.

Or will be, she reflected.

Lizina still had a few loose ends to tie. Loose ends with names. Thax Wilanu. Mikk, Kukis, and Degula. Ganesa of Resh was no longer on her mental list (thank you, Dorjan). Oh, she intended to make certain that the Diamond Lady of the space-traveling brothel no longer sailed the spaceways. Ganesa was one loose end she would not leave dangling.

Drawing another lung-filling breath, she waved at a line of yellow and orange cabs parked across the curving concourse that ran in front of the terminal. The taxi at the head of the queue lifted from the ground. It cut across the traffic to halt before the copper-haired woman and her young companion.

The rear door to the cab swung upward. Pulling Chane after her, Lizina climbed in. For a brief instant, her beaming face sobered. She glanced at the driver's registration and attached hologram which hung beside the floater's control console.

Luck was not with her. The hologram was not of Mikk.

She hadn't expected it to be. Just hoped. It would have moved her plans along at a faster pace, that was all. But then, Lizina did not intend to rely on luck. She would succeed where fickle luck would only fail.

"Dasha Concourse, Branch Alamea F-7," she instructed the driver as she settled back in the seat. Then she amended, "Forget the tube. Go through the city."

"It'll cost ya more. Rush traffic this time of day," a tired, monotone voice replied.

"Through the city," Lizina repeated. "My friend's never seen Harmony. And it's been a long time for me."

"Through the city it is, lady." The voice sounded three times as tired as it had a moment before.

The taxi lifted and swerved onto the concourse. Neither Lizina nor Chane noticed the driver's overt lack of caution. Chane's attention was riveted to the woman beside him and her enthusiastically pointing finger that darted from one window to another while she gave a running travelogue of landmarks passed.

It had been Lizina's intention to drive directly to the Harith Estate. That intention changed the instant she saw the twin spires of the Harmony CredExchange, a bank on whose board her former husband Garold Harith had sat for ten years.

She ordered the driver to park in front of the bank. When he did, she told him to wait until she returned. His questioning expression was assuaged by the roll of stells Lizina tossed in the front seat (the last of her Mirjer money).

Once more grabbing Chane's arm, she tugged him after her through the cyber-automated doors of the Harmony CredExchange. Ten minutes later she stood within the office of the bank president. So did four of the institution's top officers. Chane glanced at her. Definitely impressed by the service she received.

There was a myriad of questions about her abrupt disappearance after Garold's death. (All pleasantly posed and not *too* probing. After all, she was still a major stockholder in the bank.)

She deftly fielded the inquiries with the brief explanation that she had gone offplanet (the truth) to overcome the grief of Garold's death (a lie).

There were a couple of raised eyebrows and more than a few knowing, corner-of-the-eye glances at Chane. Other than the expected reactions, no one questioned her further.

Thirty minutes later, Lizina had gotten what she had come for. A new credcard for herself. An account for Chane (padded with a hyper-liberal cushion of stells for his services to date). And a hefty envelope of ready cash.

The latter she dropped into the cab driver's lap as she climbed into the taxi again.

"I want to rent you and your cab for the next few hours. Will that cover expenses?"

It was a frivolous waste. She had her own car (cars) at the estate. With two chauffeurs. But the Harith mansion was at least an hour's drive from the heart of Harmony. She didn't want to waste a minute of her first day home.

"For this, you've got the cab and me for the next *week*, ma'am. If you want!" The weariness was gone from the driver's voice—and face. "Just tell me where to, ma'am!"

"The next few hours will be sufficient." Lizina caught the dazed look still plastered across Chane's face. She winked coyly and turned back to the driver. "First, I want you to drive us to Tulann's. After that . . . after that, we'll see."

Tulann's was the home of Panish's ultra-est of ultra-exclusive dress designers. Tulann (a Lanatian like Lizina) catered to the upper ten per cent of Panish's highest social echelon (translation: rich). Lizina (via her inherited wealth) was in the top one per cent.

Like a child set free within a toy shop, Lizina bought.
Bought gowns. Bought dresses. Bought furs. Bought
negligees. Bought lingerie—not reelsilk but *real* silk,
sleek and cool on skin that had known only the coarse-
ness of a jumpsuit for months. And she bought acces-
sories for all of it.

She bought and bought, then bought more. And when
her hunger was partially sated, she took a Jahpurese-
rust suede (real) suit, triple-ruffle-collar silk (real) blouse,
and a pair of high-heeled, sharp-toed Saipese lizard
boots (equhyde—more durable than leather and the ma-
terial *breathed*) and walked into a dressing room.

Her back to three angled full-length mirrors, Lizina
ran a finger down the front of her jumpsuit. Molecular
binding opened. She tossed her shoulders and wiggled
the suit over her hips.

She took the ugly Mirjer attire from the floor and
stuffed it into the flight bag with its identical tan companion. Sealing the bag (a gesture of soul-felt finality),
she tossed it into a disposal chute.

A grin spread across her face when a white glow
flared about the chute's mouth. Her last souvenirs of
Mahir and Mirjam were now reduced to recyclable base
molecules.

She turned to the mirrors. After close inspection of
her nakedness, she nodded to the reflection. Even the
last traces of Mahir's cruelly inflicted bruises had faded
from her golden tan body.

The mental and emotional bruises would take longer
to dissipate.

With deliberate slowness, she dressed. She luxuriated
in the exquisite texture of each piece of clothing she
donned. The feel of it to her palms and fingers. The
way it caressed the smoothness of her limbs. She felt
like an artist creating an animated soft-sculpture.

Creation complete, she posed before the mirrors while
she turned first one way and then the other. Again she

nodded her approval at the women reflected in the mirrors.

She even liked her hair, despite the fact that she hadn't visited a stylist in months. The sleek copper-hued strands cascaded about her shoulders in a soft inward flip. While not glamorous, it was attractive. And there was a certain indefinable no-nonsense statement in its simplicity.

Lizina nodded again. She approved of the image she presented. It corresponded to what she felt—had to feel, to achieve what she intended.

She pivoted, glanced over her shoulder to the mirrors one last time, winked, and walked back into Tulann's lounge-decorated showroom.

Chane sat engrossed in a willowy raven-haired beauty who modeled the latest of ultra-erotic negligees for two hopeful matrons. He glanced up at Lizina. He did a classic double-take. His lips puckered in a silent whistle of total approval.

Credcard to Tulann herself, receipt signed, Chane loaded with boxes and packages, Lizina—feeling like a caterpillar transformed to soar-flitting butterfly—led her burdened companion back to the waiting taxi. The driver's eyes came to attention. She directed him to Ezhno-Ezhno (the masculine equivalent of Tulann's).

"Yes, *madam*!"

The proprietor offered no complaints at the two hours after closing required to outfit Chane with a complete wardrobe. He simply smiled widely (perhaps more widely than Tulann) and accepted Lizina's credcard and signature on the receipt, wished them a pleasant evening, and carried half of Chane's new burden out to the cab personally.

From Ezhno-Ezhno, Lizina told the cabbie to take them to the *Lal Autar*. Her voice did not betray the timidity that set her heart pounding within her chest.

Lal Autar was the most exclusive club in Harmony—

on all of Panish. It was also where she had met Thax
Wilanu. There Thax had slipped her a Sleeper disguised
as an antintoxicant. In a glass of champagne. She had
passed out in Mikk's cab and awakened on the deck of
Forerunner—slave to Captain Kukis.

It took a deep steadying breath to get her past the
club's double doors. But Lizina entered. It was an act
of defiance. A burial rite to cleanse herself of the fears
and doubts that nibbled at her confidence. A measure
to assure herself that the past was indeed passed.

It worked. All the time the maître d' seated the
couple within the dining room, Lizina's gaze searched
the faces of the club's patrons. She hoped to find Thax.
Again luck was elsewhere. Once more she told herself
that she would have no need of luck.

Cold, methodical calculation would serve better.

Dinner arrived, rich to palate and credaccount. Lizina
and Chane (dazed by the world of wealth surrounding
him) thoroughly enjoyed every bite. Then relished each
drop of dessert: Candied Lanatian Creme aflame with
Qalaran brandy.

Definitely satisfied and feeling pampered, Lizina and
Chane left *Lal Autar*. Before releasing the driver from
his temporary employment, Lizina directed him to the
Harith Estate. Wearing a smile from here to there, he
drove. Carefully.

Thirty minutes later and after three trips to and from
the cab to unload the packages, Lizina led Chane into
the opulence of the Harith Mansion. It took another two
hours to explain away her disappearance to the servants—
whose presence surprised Lizina until she realized that
Garold had often been gone for months at a time and
arranged for their salaries to be paid by his attorney.
She had never canceled those arrangements. Then the
mistress of Harith gave Chane a guided tour through the
three stories and two sub-basements of her home.

When at last they slid into Lizina's emperor-sized

bed, they made love. Long, and slow, and mutually satisfying.

Lizina smiled as she snuggled close to Chane's warmth and sleepily closed her eyes. It had been a long day. And O such a marvelous way to return to Panish!

Her single regret was that it was Chane who lay beside her and not Dorjan. That, however, would change. She intended to see to it personally.

7

Breakfast came in bed. Served by a cyberbutler, proving that Lizina's servants understood discretion.

Chane ravenously busied himself with three Golden Coin Eggs afloat in rich oyster sauce, sweet rice, and strips of smoked fish. Lizina poked a fork at her plate. Occasionally she nibbled. Never tasting the feast that had been prepared for her first morning home.

The problem was that she was home—not in HOME.

Dorjan. Where are you now? When . . .

She tried not to ponder the possibility of when *Misfit* would dock at Panishport and bring Dorjan to her. It only made the waiting worse.

Do I have to wait?

She pushed the errant thought aside. What did she know of plying the spaceways?

And yet!

Other women are spacefarers. Captain their own ships. Bururia. Hellfire. Oh yes, and . . . Ganesa.

The concept of her—Lizina Harith—seated before the console of a spacer was ludicrous. Yet the image would not fade. It was the blossom of a seed she had carried with her for months.

A spaceship offered her an avenue to return to HOME—and other things. Items on the mental accounting list she kept that had to be balanced before she left Panish. With or without Dorjan.

Lizina took a birdlike bite of sauce-dripping egg. She

rolled it in her mouth, unaware of its pleasing texture or ultra-rich flavor. Her brain was elsewhere. Her mind roamed the stars.

Chane leaned to the left and placed his emptied breakfast tray on the floor. Hands locked behind a head of thick black hair, he sank into the pillows propped behind his back. A contented sigh came from his chest and throat.

"I don't know when I died and went to nirvana. But praise be to Booda." He chuckled and sighed again.

"And to think that you almost decided to continue home rather than coming with me." Lizina gazed at the handsome young man beside her in the ridiculously large bed.

"Hey, I managed to sign up for a two-year hitch mining on Mirjam. No one ever said anything about me being intelligent!" He laughed and stretched lazily. "To be honest, all this seems just one fantastic dream. I'm afraid I'll wake any moment to find myself still stuck in Ore City."

"It's no dream," Lizina assured him. "Everything you see is all quite real."

"I know." His head rolled toward her, gaze caressing her partially exposed warheads.

Chane's impish grin transformed into the uncertain awe she had seen on his face during the wild shopping spree yesterday. "It really *is* hard to believe. In Ore City I never imagined any of this. You were . . . I mean . . ."

He stammered. His gaze darted away from her in embarrassment.

"In Ore City I was a whore." She stared at him.

Chane's eyes rose to Lizina again. He looked like a boy (not a man) struggling with guilt and shame for an innocently made social blunder.

"That's what I was." Lizina smiled gently. "It wasn't

of my own choosing, but I *was* a hust. There's nothing either you or I can do to change what I was."

He took her hand, squeezed, and pressed it to his lips.

"Lizina, I didn't mean anything. You know how I feel about you. I just . . ."

"Shhhhh," she hushed him. "I know you didn't mean anything. If I thought you did, you'd be on the floor with this tray atop your head."

From the subtle shifting of Chane's expression, she realized that he knew she meant what she said.

She did. She had been used for the last time. It wasn't going to happen again. *Never!*

"Don't get too accustomed to luxury." Her voice softened, as did Chane's expression. "I told you I had work for you here. I have. How hard it will be, I'm not sure. But I expect you to earn the exorbitant salary I intend to pay you. Understand?"

Chane nodded.

"No, you don't." Lizina shook her head. "I'm not sure I do. But I've got some ideas I want you to listen to. Then tell me if I'm as crazy as I think I am."

"I'm listening."

Lizina took a deep breath and began. She tried to place her random thoughts into an organized outline at first; then she stopped bothering and let them flow out as they came to her.

She carefully watched her young employee/lover. More than a few questioning furrows rumpled his brow and Lizina did not miss an occasional doubtful raising of eyebrows. But he listened, never commenting until she had verbally committed the thoughts that had been scurrying undefined in her mind for months.

She looked at him and shrugged in question.

Chane leaned back and stared at the ceiling. He lay there for a several long, heavy moments before he nodded, more to himself than Lizina.

"I have no doubt that you're a total lunatic—mad as a rabid grat!" he finally said. "Only someone whose personality had gone one hundred per cent frag would even contemplate the things you've just said. Let alone actually consider doing them."

He rolled to his side, facing her. His expression was that of a man now, all serious and sincere, without trace of his boyish innocence.

"And I also know, you damn' well intend to try everything you mentioned. Whether I'm with you or not."

Lizina didn't reply. He was right. She was going to do everything she had said. Or kill herself trying.

Which was not beyond the very real realm of possibility.

"So, it comes to me that I have two choices. One: do what any sane man would do and get the hell out before I get myself killed." Chane's voice was somber. "Two: stay here with you, and watch both of us get killed."

Still Lizina said nothing.

"The trouble with number one is that I would never be able to live with myself when I finally heard you'd killed yourself . . . without me there helping you any way I could. Not that I'm sure I can help!

"So . . . that leaves number two, Lizina. If you're going to kill yourself, I'm going to be there to help." He squeezed her hand again. "Go ahead and call your attorney and set up an appointment. You're not going to be satisfied until you get things moving."

Joyously she threw her arms about his neck (messily depositing her breakfast tray and its contents on the carpeted floor without so much as noticing the racket). Her mouth covered his.

Chane returned the embrace and filled her mouth with tongue, easing her down into the bed. Her hands did the rest, bringing his sleeping slicer wide awake, then guiding him atop her and into the welcoming haven of her body.

He smiled when their lips reluctantly parted. His weight held on propped elbows, he gazed impishly down into the beauty of her delicate face. Their bodies rocked in a mutually increasing rhythm.

"Is this . . . the way I'm . . . supposed to earn that . . . exorbitantly high . . . salary you've promised me?"

"This is just a (uh!) fringe benefit. Guaranteed to promote a better (ah!) employee-employer relationship. *Ohh*."

When his lips opened to reply, she hushed him with a kiss. Her hands tightened on his buttocks, drawing him deeper into her liquid warmth. There was no need for further words and soon there was neither inclination nor time for anything so dull as talking.

And awhile later, still side by side in bed, Lizina called the Harith family attorney (minus visual transmission). Chane had been wrong. She had been satisfied before making the call. Very satisfied.

Pain twisted the face of Yemahl Huhleem (senior member of Huhleem, Sudi, Tabir, Yutu, Kwam & Progeny). The sleek attorney took on the appearance of a man beset by an unexpected attack of gas.

"Lizina . . ." he began, then paused. His voice was two octaves above its normal range. He cleared his throat, swallowed, and tried again. "Lizina, certainly you aren't serious? Liquidate so many assets to effectuate purchase of a . . . a . . . *spacecraft*?"

"Very serious."

Lizina ignored the amused smile that tugged up the corners of Chane's mouth. She had expected her wishes to be questioned, even argued. Yemahl's obvious pained distress was unforeseen.

"Musla, why?" The attorney stared at her as though incapable of comprehending the request.

"I see no reason to explain my wishes. If you can't handle the matter, I'll find someone who can."

A doubly pained expression spread over the lawyer's pampered face. Garold Harith and his estate had been with the firm since Garold had come to Harmony to make his fortune. Any attorney onplanet would give a cube (no, both cubes) to manage the fortune.

"It's not a matter of being unable to carry out your wishes," Yemahl said, his voice still higher than normal. "I simply can't understand why you would want another spaceship?"

Another spaceship?

It was Lizina's turn to look puzzled. From that expression Huhleem took new confidence.

"You husband was the majority owner of eight spacers at the time of his death, including a private craft—*Windrammer*—which is docked at Panishport this very moment." The lawyer's manicured nails flashed as he tapped several keys on his desk console. The computer monitor to his left blipped. "This is a list of his other spacefaring vessels—your vessels. Among them are two Four-A class freighters which run between Galaxy Center and the Rim Worlds."

"I didn't know," Lizina mumbled through a sort of dazed shock.

She didn't. Garold had never discussed business during their six months together. She wasn't even sure just how wealthy she was.

Eight spacers. And two are big *ships!*

Her mind boggled. Even while they talked, Garold's private ship was berthed at Panishport! *Her* private spacer.

"This *Windrammer*, Yemahl . . . is it equipped with updated tachyon conversion systemry?" she asked a bit timidly. "And is there a crew?"

"Yes, to your first question. No, to the second. When you abruptly . . . uh . . . left Panish and could not be located, I felt it wise to dismiss the crew to cut overhead. The trained personnel required for a spaceship is an expensive item to maintain indefinitely. Even true fortunes such as yours should not be *wasted*, Lizina."

Lizina nodded, attempting to accustom herself to the fact that she—*she*—already owned a spacer. (*Eight!*) "Then I would like you to locate someone to assume the position of *Windrammer*'s captain. A discreet someone who is willing to train a green crew."

"Then I am to assume that *Windrammer* will fill your needs?" Yemahl was absolutely all attentiveness. After the shock she had given him, he was regaining his sleek appearance and smooth manner. After all, he had century upon century of lawyerish superiority to uphold.

Again Lizina nodded.

Without so much as a raised eyebrow to question her need for a "discreet" captain, Yemahl said, "I will arrange for the interviews of prospective employees. Shall I conduct the interviews personally?"

Lizina shook her head. "No. I'll interview them. The sooner the better."

She purposely neglected to mention that it would be a short-lived position. But one that would pay well. Discretion came at a high price.

"It will take two or three days to arrange the interviews." Yemahl's fingers tapped the keyboard again, apparently making a note of her wishes. "Now, what else may I assist you with, Lizina?"

Lizina took a breath to dispel a sudden wave of hesitance. "I need information on certain people. And I would prefer that their investigation not be linked with me."

Again Yemahl offered not so much as an arched eyebrow. "We have a small staff of investigators who will handle the matter. Could I have the names of the individuals and any other information that might aid in the investigation?''

She gave him the names she carried on her mental list—Thax Wilanu, Mikk, Kukis, Degula, and Ganesa (just to be certain The Diamond Lady had not escaped Forty Per Cent City). She was relieved that the attorney did not question her reasons for wanting the information.

Not, she mused, *that I'd give them to him.*

When Yemahl had finished coding her remarks into the computer, he turned to her again. ''Is there anything else?''

''One additional item. I want to buy some slaves. Five of them. It doesn't matter if they're male or female— just healthy and relatively young.''

While Yemahl didn't bat an eye, Lizina noted the shock and disgust that shadowed Chane's face. She smiled.

She hadn't discussed the purchase of slaves with Chane. Hadn't thought of it until a moment ago, actually. Now all she had to do was to wait and see if it *worked.*

8

The cat paused in its leisurely stroll across the neatly manicured lawn. Its great head, tufted at the jowls with red-tinged fur, lifted. The inverted triangle of black that was its nose quivered, sniffing the air. Black-slitted eyes ringed by pale green irises shifted their nocti-luminescent stare from one side of the spacious yard to the other.

The head lowered and the cat moved on.

From behind the fanned fronds of a bushy greenwing, Dorjan watched the cat disappear behind the two-story house. He released an overly held breath.

A similar sigh of tension came from Songan, crouched behind the twisted trunk of a tree to Dorjan's left.

The great cat was a Lung Pao—a Dragon Panther of Saiping. Standing a meter at the shoulders and weighing upwards to one hundred-thirty kilos, a Lung Pao was a dangerous adversary.

Doubly dangerous. The Lung Pao was a genetically engineered breed. A feline with chromosomes subtly manipulated for boosted intelligence. Although a long, long way from HRal, the Dragon Panthers of Saiping were semi-sentient.

They were also as alien to the jungle planet Ginneh as were the smooth-cut lawn and the house it surrounded. None of the three belonged amid the sweltering rain forest. Yet they were here.

And they were the reason Dorjan and his fellow Harbian hid amid the jungle's underbrush.

Within the house (beyond the five Dragon Panthers and ten armed guards constantly patrolling the grounds) lived Mensah Nav. Nav was chief administrator for the cyprium mining concern on Ginneh. It was one more holding of TMSMCo.

That in itself was of little concern to the captain of *Misfit*. Or to his crew.

What was of import was the fact that Nav had purchased the Akil woman Kefira altRusalka from Ganesa of Resh. Kefira was now being held within the house. A slave to Mensah Nav.

In the week Dorjan and crew had been onplanet (minus the Jarp Songbird who remained onboard the orbiting *Misfit*), they had seen Kefira only from a distance. Twice daily the alien woman was brought outside for a stroll about the grounds at all times surrounded by four guards. Dorjan had discovered no way to snatch her safely away during the walks.

Nor had a method for gaining access to the house presented itself to *Misfit*'s captain.

Ten armed guards and five Lung Pao were formidable obstacles to overcome—even for a man known as The Shadow Walker.

Two guards stepped from behind the house. Both carried plasma pistols. Stoppers were strapped to their waists. (Dorjan had no doubt the guns were set on Three—to kill). The only outsiders on these grounds were intruders. To Mensah Nav, intruders were enemies, and thus fair game.

The pair walked to the jungle bordering the estate in ultramarine and olive. They talked as they began to circle the perimeter of the clearing. Two friends, with a dull job.

Ten minutes from now another pair of guards would complete their circuit. It was like precision clockwork.

The random factor was provided by the Dragon Panthers. They roamed where and when they chose.

For the past week the four members of *Misfit*'s crew had alternated their reconnaissance of Nav's home. Varnalgeran Yuw and Edrek had the day watch, while Dorjan and Songan stood the night. The guards and great cats were always there. The pattern never varied.

Fingers nudged Dorjan's shoulder.

"It's getting close to dawn. We need to start back toward Deephole."

Dorjan nodded. But instead of sinking into the jungle's dense vegetation, he looked back toward Mensah Nav's two-story home.

There has to be a way in there. There has to be!

A whirl of twin rotary-blades hummed behind them. Dorjan and Songan turned. The headlights of an approaching vehicle cut through barren patches among the jungle's foliage.

"Here it comes again." Songan tilted his head toward a hovervan that moved above a rough dirt road to their left. "It's the same van."

It was. Even in the darkness, there was no mistaking the bright red vehicle. Nor the broad dent on the driver's door.

Every other night for a week, they had seen the van approach the house. Just before dawn, every time. Its purpose for making the five-klom drive from Deephole remained as unknown as what lay behind the white synthestone walls of Nav's home.

The hovervan pulled in front of the house. The driver sat within until Mensah Nav walked from the front door of the house to escort him inside. It was the same procedure Dorjan had watched on three previous occasions.

"We need to let Varn tackle that van," Songan whispered. "No one in Deephole seems to know anything about *any* red van—on this planet or any other!"

"Deephole's residents have a lack of knowledge about

a great number of things." Dorjan made no attempt to repress his disgust with Ginneh and the inhabitants of its sole city.

The truth was, not even Yuw had made any headway in locating the van or its owner. A singular blow to the Outie's ego. Varn could usually obtain information from a granite slab, if the situation warranted.

Dorjan pushed to his feet. His legs were stiff from too many nights of squatting in the darkness and straining his eyes—to see nothing.

"Let's get back to town. Edrek and Varn can have this place for another day."

Songan nodded and rose. Dorjan began the weaving five-klom walk back to the mining town.

The trek depressed Dorjan. The heat, the jungle, the smell of decaying vegetation pressed in around him. It was as if they sensed his failure to find a way into Nav's house and mocked him.

Which of course, was ridiculous. He knew that. It was just that knowing it didn't help.

Ginneh, with its heat and constantly high humidity, was slowly getting to him. And to the others. Irritation walked tall among his crew. Bickering had replaced their usual jovial conversation.

"Hold it." Songan grasped his captain's shoulder.

"What is it?" Irritation crept into Dorjan's voice, despite his attempt to contain it.

Songan shook his head. "I don't know. I thought I heard something."

Dorjan listened. Only the jungle's night sounds surrounded him.

"And I think Ginneh is eating at you as bad as it's getting to me." Dorjan started toward Deephole again.

"Maybe you're right." Songan's head turned from side to side. "But damn it, Dorjan, I'm certain I heard something."

Dorjan halted a second time. He listened and still heard nothing more than the usual sounds of Ginneh's night.

"What was it?"

"A rustle, like something moving through the brush."

Dorjan glanced about them. The jungle was still. Ultramarine fronds hung like motionless tongues.

"Come on. Some food, a shower and a few hours sleep will take the edge off."

Songan nodded—and froze.

"There it is again!"

This time Dorjan heard it. Behind them! Something *was* moving through the dense underbrush, and stealthily.

"Cut toward the road. Whatever it is, I'd rather face it in the open." Dorjan's hand went to the stopper strapped to his waist.

(He was unaccustomed to the weapon's weight. Usually he shunned weapons. So did his crew, because they were his crew. But on Ginneh—faced with a nightly five-klom stroll through the jungle—he had foregone his usual distaste for a sidearm. Now the pistol gave him a sense of security.)

The rustle came again. Closer. Moving faster.

The two crewmates hastened their own steps in an effort to reach the road. Time and again, they glanced behind them. Nothing was there but the jungle darkness.

The thundering roar came not from behind, but directly in front of them. With it was a shadow that launched itself from the other shadows of the night. A shadow that slammed into Songan's chest, throwing him to the ground.

Dorjan pivoted as a second shadow hurled itself from behind. Realization of what had occurred drove into his brain like a cold steely spike. They had been trapped. Neatly herded into an ambush.

Not by men—by Dragon Panthers!

While one slowly pressed them from the rear, the second had waited ahead.

One hundred and thirty kilos of great cat hammered into Dorjan's side. He went down like a man struck by a runaway floater. He rolled. The Lung Pao rolled with him. Recurved claws raked out. In a single swipe, the back of Dorjan's shirt was transformed to ribbons.

His flesh was spared the same fate. The cat's claws scraped harmlessly over the unipolymer plasteel wings compactly folded against his back (thank you, Murrah an Rahmyne).

He twisted in the opposite direction. He groped for his stopper, hand closing about the handle. The cylindrical gun popped free of its first holster clamp. The second . . .

Then it flew through the air as one of the Lung Pao's hind legs kicked up. Claws dug into the back of his hand. Ripping. The sticky warmth of his own blood ran between Dorjan's fingers.

He rolled again. Writhed and kicked, in a desperate attempt to shake free of the great feline. He couldn't. He did manage to wiggle about and face the animal.

Three-sem long claws slid from his fingertips. Wedging his injured right hand under the Dragon Panther's jaw, he clamped its throat with his own clawed fingers. He shoved, edging back the fanged death that snapped at his throat.

Dorjan's left hand swiped across the animal's face.

The Lung Pao screamed. No longer did yellow-green eyes glare from its slitted sockets. The cat no longer had eyes; there were only the sockets.

The scream died abruptly.

Dorjan's left hand joined his right. He ripped at the monster's throat. Again. Again. Blood gushed, and this time it was the cat's blood. Hot and wet, it soaked the frayed remnants of Dorjan's shirt. Their blood mingled, but not in brotherhood.

The big cat went limp, powerful muscles abruptly flaccid. The heat of its breath no longer bathed Dorjan's face. Its fangs were still, its claws motionless. The Lung Pao had found strength and a set of claws to best its own. It was dead.

Shoving the carcass from him, Dorjan staggered to his feet. To his right, Songan was on the ground pinned beneath his feline assailant. The former gladiator's hands were locked about the Lung Pao's throat.

Not even those powerful hands could crush the monster's gullet. The slavering fanged mouth edged closer to Songan's face with each heartbeat.

The vibe-knife that was the fingernail of Dorjan's left forefinger hummed to life. He threw himself atop the cat's broad back. Inward through thick, shaggy fur the mini-blade slid, and flesh, and bone. It struck home, slicing through vertebrae and the spinal cord they protected.

The Lung Pao went limp under Dorjan. It had joined its hunting partner in death.

Rolling from the dead cat, Dorjan tugged its carcass off Songan. The other Harbian rose to his knees. His right hand clutched at four stripe-like ribbons of red opened on his left shoulder.

"It hurts, but it's not deep," Songan assured him. "I was lucky. I saw him before he hit. I rolled with him."

Dorjan nodded. *Roll with the punches. The first rule of martial arts or street fighting—or jungle survival.*

"You?"

"My right hand. I don't know how bad it is. If it hadn't been for my wings, I'd be dead now." Dorjan stood, feeling a momentary weakness as adrenaline dissipated.

He peered at his hand. In the darkness he couldn't tell how bad it was. It did hurt like hell. And there was blood, a lot of blood.

"I better get you back to Deephole. We both need patching up." Songan moved toward his friend.

"Wait. There's something that needs to be done first."

Dorjan bent over the beast that had attacked Songan. His left hand, claws extended, rose and fell. Six times.

He moved to the dead cat that had hit him from the side and repeated the process. It was dirty work, but Dorjan knew it was necessary.

His chest heaving as he gulped for air, he stood once more. "There. When Nav's men come looking for their lost cats, they'll find them here—ripped to shreds by each other."

Songan nodded his approval. Great cats, even semisentient ones, fought among themselves. The result was often death.

Without looking back to the bleeding carcasses, Dorjan started toward Deephole. The five kloms stretched light-years before him in the night.

9

Varnalgeran Yuw methodically shook the cannister for the required thirty seconds. Forefinger atop white nozzle, he aimed at the back of Dorjan's right hand and pressed down.

An almost invisible mist spewed from the can. Cool, very cool moisture settled atop the injured hand. Back and forth, Yuw worked the spray to cover the wound. One application complete, he repeated the process. Then once more for good measure.

"It feels better already." Dorjan nodded his approval.

The topical anesthetic contained in the NueSkin had begun to work. The firebrand embedded in his flesh numbed to a glowing ember within seconds. A few moments later the pain had lessened to a dull throb.

While Yuw administered the dually effective (antiseptic and rapid healing) compound to Songan's shoulder, Dorjan studied his injury. The soothing mist went on invisibly. That state lasted only momentarily.

The back of the injured hand now appeared to be coated with a patch of snow (whiter than white atop the subcutaned blackness of Dorjan's dyed skin). Around the fringes of the whiteness, traces of color crept into the NueSkin. Within a half hour, the patch would match the hue of his flesh—perfectly.

Dorjan cautiously flexed his hand. He winced. The pain flared anew.

"Let it be!"

Dorjan glanced up. Varn stood with hands reprimand-ingly planted on his hips. He arched a disapproving eyebrow.

"You're damned lucky that was all the damage done. Now you're acting like some kid, trying to make it worse. It'll be at least two days before it feels normal. Four before it's healed. Give the NueSkin a chance to do its stuff!"

Dorjan grinned sheepishly and nodded. Varn turned and gave Songan the same threatening gaze to let him know the warning went for Mate as well as captain.

Behind the Outie's back, Dorjan winked at his fellow Harbian—and impatient patient. If he had been acting childish, Varn had more than a touch of the mother hen within him.

The Outreacher was also right. He and Songan had been lucky. His hand, though bloody and so painful he wished it belonged to someone else, was not seriously damaged. The skin had been terribly mangled but bone, vein, and muscle were left intact.

The same was true of Songan's shoulder.

A shiver ran through *Misfit*'s captain. Chill, bony fingers that tickled up and down his spine—the fear of what might have been. A prickly sensation needled at every sem of his body.

The encounter with the two Lung Pao could have been bad. Terminal. In retrospect, it appeared impossi-ble that either of them had survived. Dorjan felt not pride but almost a dizziness; elation.

"Now, you two get some sleep," Varn said in his same motherly tone. "Edrek and I have the day watch on Nav's house to attend."

"No." Dorjan shook his head. "It could only be a waste of time."

Yuw looked at his captain. His expression formed his unspoken question.

"When Nav's guards find those two dead cats, they're

going to be edgy.'' Dorjan slumped back into his chair. He felt bone-weary and in need of at least three month's sleep. ''It won't be safe for anyone coming within a klom of the place.''

''But Kefira's in that house!'' The new voice was Edrek's. He stood by the door to the cramped hotel room. ''I'm not just going to abandon her!''

''Nobody said anything about abandoning Kefira!'' Songan's words were sharp with edge. His face betrayed the same weariness and frustration Dorjan felt.

''We'll get Kefira.'' Dorjan looked back to the young Lanatian. ''I promised you that, Edrek. We'll get her.''

Somehow. He hoped.

Edrek was unsatisfied. He stood at the door glaring at his captain and friend. He looked ready to take on a Dragon Panther. Two.

The lean Lanatian's love was showing, along with his youth. Dorjan felt a strong bond with Edrek, now. Both had found women to share their lives. Ganesa of Resh had stolen those women from them. That Ganesa was repaid did not replace the loss.

Still, both women lived. Lizina was safe on Panish by now. And Kefira was here on Ginneh. The Akil woman lived. Dorjan knew that he could not vouch for her safety. He could only guess at her treatment within Nav's house, and he did not care to ponder the ways she had been used.

''We've done all we can by keeping Nav's home under surveillance,'' Songan said, his voice gentled with understanding. ''There's no way just to walk into that house and walk away with Kefira.''

''There's no sane way for us to get into that house.'' Varn plopped down on the edge of a bed. ''Even minus two Dragon Panthers, Nav's home is a fortress.''

''However, there may be an insane way to get within the house.''

That was Songan.

Three heads turned to *Misfit*'s tattooed Mate.

"I can't promise anything good, but it's the only avenue I see open to us. It'll mean going in blind . . . playing everything by ear once we're inside."

He paused, his gaze meeting the eyes of his companions one at a time.

"Let's have it," Dorjan said.

If there were a way into Nav's home, even a slim one, he would put his money on the encephaloboosted genius of his friend. As the Demon Cat, he had done so for eight years.

Songan leaned forward, wincing when he moved his injured shoulder.

"As I said, what I have in mind is insane, but then no one has ever accused *Misfit*'s crew of being sane. What we'll have to do is this, and *listen*."

He outlined his plan, and provided minute details. Dorjan could only guess at how long the tattooed giant had been mulling it over in his mind. He had never mentioned it to anyone. But then Songan worked that way. Only when a scheme was fully realized in his genius-level brain did he reveal what he intended.

"That's it." Songan sank back in his chair. "Only mad men would consider it." He did not smile.

Dorjan glanced at his companions. Each wore a smug little smile. *The smiles of madmen*, Dorjan thought, returning those smiles. Edrek and Yuw nodded at him. In turn, Dorjan nodded to his Mate.

"If it's settled, I suggest Varn and Edrek hit the streets again. Anything—*anything*—you can dig up will help." Songan's eyes rolled toward the bed. "Meanwhile, I intend to sleep. So why doesn't everyone redshift and let me do just that!"

"A dam' good idea." Dorjan rose and walked to the door. "We'll go over everything again this evening."

"We've got three days. We'll go over it a hundred times before we move. Now, good night!"

Dorjan tipped an imaginary hat and left *Misfit*'s First Mate to a well-deserved rest. While he walked to his room for at least eight hours of the same, Varn and Edrek hit Deephole's streets once again.

Bodi Halian maneuvered the red hovervan at a trundling run along the serpentinely twisting jungle road. Mud rained in droplets to each side of the car. Ginneh's skies had opened to dump an ocean into the forest this night.

Bodi didn't mind. He whistled while he drove.

Others might bitch and bicker about Ginneh and its steamy heat, the insects, and the isolation. Not Bodi Halian. He liked Ginneh. No other planet among the thirty he had seen had been so good to him.

Oh sure, Mensah Nav wasn't an easy man to work for. But Bodi knew Nav's quirks and how to stay on the man's good side. It was simple. Just do what Nav said—on his time schedule—and everything went as smooth as reelsilk. Smoother.

As easy as slicing a piece of cake. Bodi grinned. *As soft as a hust's warheads.*

Certainly there were friendlier planets than Ginneh in the galaxy. But there were very few (if any) where he could clear a kilostell a week for carrying two small boxes from Nav's home to a shuttleport five kloms away!

He didn't even mind the crazy hours Nav required. He was actually beginning to enjoy these early morning drives. There was something nice about floating along in a world that was still asleep.

And, of course, he never asked what was in the two boxes he hauled every two days. Oh sure, he wondered, but Bodi Halian was careful to let it go no further. It was better not to know. He simply picked the boxes up and delivered them.

Bodi's off-key tune grew louder.

Pos, Ginneh's been damned good to me.

His hands gently edged the guidelev to the right, then sharply pulled it to the left. The van edged around a ninety-degree turn in the road.

Flain! I could make this drive with my eyes closed!

His self-praise ended abruptly. His left foot hit the brake pedal. Forward jets flared from the vehicle's blunt snout. The twin rotors beneath the van whined as they went into reverse.

The van dipped forward. Momentum and motion were overcome. The vehicle floated a half meter from the ground, hovering.

Bodi peered out through the windscreen. Blinked and rubbed his eyes to assure himself that this wasn't a hallucination. (Ginneh booze was weak. Those who distilled it too often mixed other chemical agents with the alcohol, for added kick. And Bodi had had a couple of drinks before starting his run. It was no more than his usual procedure.)

The floater-bike remained. It lay overturned in the middle of the narrow, dirt road. Judging from the twisted chrome and bent rotor blades, it had overturned several times before coming to a halt, half-buried in the mud.

The rider?

Bodi's right hand twisted a knob on the control console. The van's headlamps brightened and shifted from side to side, eerie swerving eyes probing the dimness, scanning the road.

There! Ten meters beyond the twisted wreckage. A man, lying face down in the mud. He wore a black jumpsuit. The same as those worn by Nav's guards.

Bodi tapped two yellow glowing buttons atop the console. The whine of the rotors lowered in pitch. Gently, the hovervan floated to the ground. The engines hummed soft now, idling.

If this were one of Nav's men . . .

Bodi needed no more. The mere chance was enough. To help Mensah Nav was to help himself.

Leaving the engine running, Bodi thumbed his door open and stepped into Ginneh's night—and mud.

That was his first and only mistake. The three men who stepped from the jungle (stoppers leveled at his chest) gave him no chance for others.

"Varn, Edrek, move the bike and let's get out of here." Dorjan waved an arm toward the wreckage.

While Edrek pulled himself from the mud, Varnalgeran Yuw trotted to the overturned floater-bike.

"You, back into the van."

Songan prodded Bodi's ribs with the muzzle of his pistol. He kept the weapon trained on the man until Dorjan moved around the hovervan and climbed into the seat beside him.

Under the directions of the black-skinned man at his side, Bodi raised the van's rear hatch. The three remaining hijackers piled in.

"Now, drive," Dorjan ordered. "Take it slow and easy and you won't get hurt. Try anything stupid, and this is set on Three."

Bodi's eyes darted a fearful glance at the stopper. It was indeed set on the kill-beam.

His fingers (less steady than they had been moments ago) tapped the two yellow buttons. The hovervan rose and edged forward—slow and easy.

While not the smartest man on Ginneh, Bodi Halian was not stupid.

Mensah Nav froze when the door to the hovervan opened and he stared into the long, cylindrical barrel of Dorjan's stopper. His dark eyes nervously flicked between the weapon and its owner. A thin-lipped mouth trembled, setting the moustache atop his upper lip aquiver like a wiggling worm.

Dorjan's gaze ran over the mine administrator. Until

now he had only glimpsed Nav from a distance. This close Mensah Nav elicited an indefinable gut reaction in the Harbian. He felt revulsion.

The black suit (Saipese in design) Nav wore was an attempt to disguise the slightness of his physique. He stood a short hundred-seventy sems and weighed no more than sixty-five kilos.

Nav's jet hair was greased slick against his head and his lips were a subcutaneous red. That lurid hue was in full conflict with the yellowish tinge of his skin—a hue normally found among the natives of Terasaki and Saiping. Yet his facial features lacked what humankind had once called an oriental cast.

His features were soft, puffy; almost flaccid. And quite devoid of character lines or wrinkles.

"In the house, or you'll end up like your friend here." Dorjan tilted his head toward the driver's seat.

Bodi lay slumped across the guidelev, looking very dead. (He wasn't. He was merely unconscious. Varnalgeran Yuw's stopper—set on two—had seen to that the moment Bodi had killed the hovervan's engines. Better to have the man unconscious and neatly tucked away in the van than for them to try to keep tabs on him.)

Nav nodded his acceptance. There was little else he could do. This accoster's pistol was on its highest setting. He had given every indication that he would use it.

When Songan had the mining official covered, Dorjan slid from the van. Face expressionless, he motioned Nav into the house. The sickly-looking man went.

Inside, Dorjan ordered him to halt. He waved Varn to the end of a long wood paneled hall—real wood. As the Outie scurried down the hallway, Nav turned to his captors.

"What do you want?"

"You have someone who belongs to us. Someone Ganesa of Resh stole," Dorjan answered, his attention split between Yuw's progress and Nav.

Puzzlement clouded the mine administrator's face. His thick eyebrows dipped downward atop his narrowed eyes. The expression was unnerving to see. Not one single crease furrowed the paleness of his brow. An instant later the uncertainty was replaced by what Dorjan could only describe as relief.

"Ah, Kefira." Nav's smile slid across his face like oil. "An exquisite creature. And rare! Well worth risking one's neck to possess. However, it is a foolish risk. You'll never get offplanet with her. I would venture to say you'll never get beyond this house again—*alive*. My guards . . ."

Varn signaled them on.

Dorjan jabbed Nav's ribs with his stopper.

"And I'll venture that not one of those guards will do a damned thing as long as we've got you with us. Now, take us to Kefira."

Nav's eyes narrowed. Anger? Realization that as long as he was their captive, he was their passport offplanet? Dorjan wasn't sure. He didn't care. He simply intended to keep Nav close. Very close.

Nodding for Edrek to join Yuw at the end of the hall, Dorjan kept Songan beside him as he directed Nav to follow *Misfit*'s two crewmates.

"How many guards in the house?" Dorjan nudged his prisoner's back with his stopper.

"Three, all upstairs. Armed with plasma pistols." Nav's gaze swerved to a flight of stairs at the end of the hall.

Dorjan nodded to Varn and Edrek. The two ducked beside the stairs and pressed flat against the wall. Their stoppers were raised and ready.

"Call them down."

Nav hesitated. Dorjan's stopper nudged again. Nav did as ordered.

A moment later the guards (three, armed with plasma

pistols) came to the head of the stairs. Dorjan nodded again.

Yuw and Edrek stepped from the wall, swung their pistols upward and squeezed. The three dropped before their eyes could widen in surprise. *Misfit*'s two crewmates raced up the stairs and stripped the unconscious men of their weapons.

"Keep the plasma guns and dump the stoppers," Dorjan called out. "Check the upper rooms. Our host might be hiding some surprises that he neglected to mention."

"For your sake, I hope you haven't," Songan added, his eyes cold dark holes that menaced Nav.

The man's eyes rolled upward. His three guards had been left where they had fallen. None of the men moved. (They did live. Of course Nav had no way of knowing that Yuw's and Edrek's stoppers had been on the second setting. They were only guards, to Mensah Nav. Hired help.)

"They were the only guards in the house. I swear! The rest are outside. Ten in all."

"And three Dragon Panthers." Songan smiled. "There used to be five."

Mensah Nav stared. His voice was an incredulous near-whisper. "You?"

Songan nodded.

Fear moved across Nav's face, mixed with awe. These men had killed two of the Lung Pao! And three guards. Not to mention the van's driver.

"It's clear up here," Edrek called down when he and Varn appeared at the head of the stairs again.

Dorjan waved them down and turned back to his prisoner. "Now where is Kefira?"

"Below." Nav swallowed hard. "The house has a single-level basement."

Dorjan jammed his stopper into the quaking bastard's belly. Nav needed no further instructions. He led the four intruders to the basement stairs at the rear of the house. Catalyzed by another jab, he moved downward ahead of his captors.

The basement was small. No more than a narrow and dim-lit corridor of bare gray synthestone that ran for six meters. One metal door stood on each side of the corridor. Both were equipped with palmlocks.

"She's in the room to the right." Nav glanced up to Dorjan.

"Then we'll try the one on the left first." Dorjan tilted his head toward the other door.

"Do you think I'm a fool? She's in there!" Nav jabbed a finger toward the right.

As the administrator of Ginneh's cyprium mines started to the rightward door, Edrek shoved him to the opposite side of the corridor.

"You heard the man! Open the left one first!"

Nav glared at the youth. Incredibly, he did not move.

The sudden astonishing display of bravado piqued Dorjan's interest. Nav had absolutely nothing to gain by this abrupt show of stubbornness. The point had to be—what had he to lose?

Dorjan nodded to his First Mate.

Songan's left hand snaked out. Like a vise it clamped about Nav's right wrist, and squeezed. The cowering swine whimpered as the pressure from those fingers steadily grew. Songan didn't give the swine a second opportunity to comply with Dorjan's command. He jerked the smaller man around and slapped his open palm against the lock.

The door on the left hissed open.

"I think you should take a look at this." Songan turned to his captain as he released Nav. "It seems this toad *was* hiding something."

Dorjan moved to the door. Inside was a small laboratory. Dorjan was certain it was not used for assaying ore samples. Two plasseal pouches of fine crimson powder lay on the edge of a table near the door.

Dorjan opened one and started to sniff its contents. Songan grabbed his arm.

"One whiff of that and you'll be on high-zap for at least eight hours. It's TZ."

Dorjan turned to Nav. Black eyes surrounded by puffy features merely glared back.

Pieces in a horrible picture tumbled into place.

SotKil had mistaken *Misfit* for a ship he had followed from Ginneh. A spacer that supposedly carried the illegal drug tetrazombase. The pirate had said this branch of the spaceways was a major artery in the black market trade of the will-robbing chemical.

Misfit and crew had accidentally traced that artery to its heart!

The guards, the Dragon Panthers weren't for Kefira. They were to protect Nav and a highly profitable TZ operation! A drug that transformed human and alien into mindless automatons.

Kefira! If this brotherslicer has used one gram of this filth on her, I'll . . .

"Damn!" Dorjan pivoted to the door on the opposite side of the narrow hallway. "Edrek, get Kefira out of there!"

Edrek grabbed Nav and jerked him to the door. Without protest Nav placed his hand on the palmlock. The door opened.

The room beyond was as sparsely decorated as the rest of the basement. It held only a bed and a sitter.

On that bed was Kefira . . . and then she was on her feet running into Edrek's arms. Tears of joy flowed from her saucer-round, golden eyes. After a flurry of kisses and hugs for her beloved Lanatian, the Akil plied a flourish of kisses and hugs on each of the *Misfit*'s crew—and captain. Then she was back in Edrek's arms, clinging tightly to her lover and rescuer.

And no, Nav had not used the drug on her.

Dorjan asked no further questions. Kefira, as was the custom of her race, believed in *makhseem*. The sharing of body and soul. If Nav had used her body, it had been without vocal protest.

There was no need for embarrassing or enraging young Edrek. While love was sometimes blind, more often it was irrational. Dorjan didn't trust Edrek's understanding of Akil customs. For now, it was enough that the two were together again.

If Edrek had half the sense he had displayed in other matters when it came to love, he would never probe into the months he and Kefira had been separated.

With a broad grin for the reunited couple and warm sensation coursing through him, the captain of *Misfit* nodded to Songan and Varn. He pointed to the TZ lab.

"Burn it! Use the plasma guns!"

He had no doubt that Nav would be back in business eventually. But destroying the laboratory would slow down TZ production temporarily, he thought, and that felt good.

Yuw and Songan stood in the doorway. They raised their stolen weapons. Actinic blue globes of energy spat from the muzzles.

A moment later, Dorjan peered over his friends' shoulders. The lab had been transformed into a blackened wreck of melted metal and glass. Dorjan nodded his approval.

"Now let's get the vug out of here."

The trio off *Misfit* turned. Nav was no longer beside them. He was running up the stairs.

Dorjan's stopper jerked up. He squeezed. An almost invisible sonic beam shot out. Too late; the man had reached the security of the house's first floor.

"Move it!" Dorjan raced toward the stairs. "The bastard's gone for his guards!"

Without looking back to his companions, Dorjan took

the stairs two at a time. He glanced around. Nav was nowhere in sight. Dorjan spotted an open rearward door. From outside he heard Nav crying for help.

"Get to the van!" Dorjan waved his crewmates to the front of the house, while he moved to the open door.

There to the right, Nav stood pointing toward the house. Two guards and a Lung Pao ran toward him from the edge of the jungle.

Stopper set to maximum, Dorjan aimed at the bounding cat. He squeezed.

The Dragon Panther jerked in mid-leap and twisted grotesquely. Then it fell to the tidily trimmed lawn. It did not move.

Heat—searing heat that radiated from a plasma bolt—bathed the right side of Dorjan's face. Energy exploded in electric fury. It took half the door with it.

Dorjan jerked back. A streak of blue flashed by him. Another plasma bolt. The wall behind him now contained a round, char-tinged door that hadn't been there an instant before.

Sucking in a deep breath, the master of *Misfit* stepped back into the open doorway. With legs wide in a defiant stance, he swung his stopper up, aimed at the first guard, and squeezed.

Without waiting to view the results of the shot, he took aim at the second man running toward him. Again he fired.

He leaped back into the house and the relative protection of the wall. His heart thudded in his chest and his temples were apound. His mouth was suddenly filled with cotton.

A blue bolt streaked through the door to burn an even larger hole into the wall.

He had missed at least one of the guards with his two quick shots, if not both. He had no intention of stepping into the line of fire again. Not armed only with a stopper.

He took the only sensible course open to him. He retreated through the house to join the others.

"Down!"

"Lie flat!"

"Keep down!"

A chorus of distressed cries greeted him as he entered the hall to the house's front entrance. Songan and Yuw knelt by the door. An explosion—the impact of a plasma bolt—came from outside. Dirt and bits of grass showered through the open door.

"What in the hell's going on?"

Misfit's First Mate and computrician looked over their shoulders to their captain. Songan spoke.

"It's Kefira and Edrek. Nav's guards have them pinned down in the van."

He didn't mention the obvious. The three of them were successfully contained within the house.

"Varn: cover the rear. Two guards with plasma guns were on the way in the back door."

The Outie responded, moving faster than a man carrying that much weight should. Dorjan slid along the wall to drop beside his fellow Harbian.

The van, rear door open, stood ten meters away. Beyond that six men, guns held before them, were advancing on the house. At best the situation appeared hopeless.

10

The needle nose of *Windrammer* slipped half a degree
to port and bobbed norward. Hoku called out the
trajectory shift as SIPACUM blinked them on the
monitor.

Lizina's hands ran over the con. Fingers dipped to
jab at the arrays of multicolored glo-buttons. Her gaze
focused on the green plate of a phosphor screen. The
pulsing " + " atop a degree-by-degree grid slipped to the
right and downward. A double zero reading flashed
across the bottom of the screen.

Windrammer was once again aligned with Panishport's
docking berth Q-5.

Releasing a breath held too long, Lizina glanced to a
mini-display just above eye level. A holographic image
of the space station hung there, relayed by *Windrammer*'s
optics. The berth lay dead ahead, a ring of red and
white lights delineating its circular mouth.

"Dammit, Harith!" A gravelly voice growled over
Lizina's right shoulder. "Stop window gazing and keep
your ship on course!"

An arm shot over her left shoulder to jab a finger at
the green monitor.

"You over-adjusted! Look at the reading! Half a
second off-line! Get your prow on target!"

Lizina's fingers tickled the controls. The 0-0 reading
flashed back on screen. This time her eyes remained on
the monitor.

"An' you!" The growling man turned to *Windrammer*'s computrician, Hoku. "Where in Musla's hell were you! Your job is to read SIPACUM to your captain! *Do it!* Don't wait for her to ask for information! Spit it out the instant SIPACUM does! Wake up, little girl! This isn't some dam' floater-car! It's a spacer! And it takes a crew to run it!"

The growl moved on to Chane. (It was a growl. Lizina had never heard the voice speak in what she could call a normal tone.)

"And Booda's ass, man! You're supposed to be Mate on this ship! You're not sitting in that chair to stop it from floating away! Earn your pay! If the computrician misses a reading, back 'er up! Today! Not next year!"

The brief silence was punctuated by a throat-rumbling, disgust-filled, "Damn!"

The growl and the disgust belonged to one Captain Bogar Kokudza. Known throughout the spaceways as the Bogey Man—along with a long list of other nicknames that usually began with expletives.

Short and stocky, Bogar's age was seventy-five yearsess, all but fifteen spent on the decks of spacers. He looked twice that. And five times as mean (which he was).

He was known for riding his crew and pushing his ships beyond their operational envelope. He was also good. Damned good. Which was why Lizina had hired him.

Officially Bogar had listed as *Windrammer*'s captain. He wasn't. He *was* a no-nonsense, hard-nosed, unrelenting training officer that drilled and grilled the spacer's crew like a man obsessed.

Lizina had given him two weeks to turn her and her untrained crew into spacefarers. Bogar intended to do just that, or kill them trying.

Two weeks was all he had. At the end of that time,

his own ship—a *big* spacer—was to be released from drydock after a series of modifications and systemry updates.

"Ten kloms out," Chane called to his captain-in-training.

Lizina hit the forward maneuvering rockets. *Windrammer*'s momentum decreased to point-oh-five.

"Bring it down to point-oh-one! We want to dock, not jar Panishport out of orbit!" Bogar's growl burned down the back of her neck.

"Oh-five is standard docking procedure!" Lizina protested.

"Some would call a quick wham-bam 'standard lovemaking procedure'!" Bogar snarled in instant reply. "But if it's slow and gentle, it's a hell of a lot more satisfying. Bring it down to *point-oh-one*!"

Lizina did.

Windrammer's prow gently slipped into the waiting maw of the docking berth. A metallic clang rang through the ship as cradling collars locked about the hull.

"Systemry check," Lizina called out, and she toed open intraship comm.

One by one *Windrammer*'s crew reported fully functional systemry. Lizina switched off each system. Her ship now lay sleeping, safely tucked in its berth. She swiveled around to face Bogar.

He sucked at his lips and shook his head. "You forgot your cargo check with the port authority."

"*Windrammer* doesn't carry cargo." Lizina stood and stretched. Every muscle in her body ached. She felt as if she had been hunched over the con for a week instead of a mere hour.

"All ships carry cargo, even the liners. Especially private spacers. It costs to sail the Tachyon Trail. A pleasure craft can make expenses by hauling cargo. Get on the comm and see what's available." Bogar jabbed a stubby finger toward the console.

Lizina's lips opened to protest. She swallowed her words (and pride) before they were formed. *Dammit! He's right! He's always right!*

And, yes, there was a shipment of medical equipment that needed to be jumped to Lanatia in two days. Lizina took the consignment.

"We make our next long flight in two days then," Bogar said when she turned back to him. "In the meanwhile, we practice. We'll pop out a few thousand kloms, maneuver, bring *Windrammer* back in. Then do it over again."

"Do it again and again and again until we get it right," Chane said under his breath.

Bogar's coal-black eyes cut to the young man. "You're doing it *right*, now! Space don't allow wrong! Those who do it the wrong way are dead! Now you're going to learn to do it perfectly! Understand?"

Chane nodded sheepishly.

"Good." Bogar looked back to Lizina. "Eight hours leave, then get them back here for another run. We'll practice maneuvering until we make the Lanatia haul."

Lizina reopened the comm and announced the schedule to her (officially Bogar's) crew. Toeing off the intraship comm, she closed her eyes and sighed.

At the moment her carefully schemed plans seemed to contain as many holes as a sieve. She had never considered the work that would be involved. The hard, minutely detailed work required to operate a spacer. To make a team out of her, Chane and five equally inexperienced slaves.

She shook her head. Hoku and her fellow crewmates were no longer slaves. Lizina had purchased them, given them freedom. She had offered them jobs onboard *Windrammer*. All had accepted and willingly submerged themselves in this new life.

What had appeared to be the perfect plan now seemed hopeless. All it was supposed to take was encephaloboosts. A few simple injections to provide the knowledge needed to run and maintain a spacer.

All seven of them had received the injections. Their brains now contained the required knowledge.

Knowledge and practical experience, however, were two entirely separate entities. The crew and captain-to-be of *Windrammer* were terribly lacking in the latter. By now Lizina wasn't at all certain that Bogar could provide everything needed in a mere two weeks.

She opened her eyes. The con lay dead except for a few lights that glowed steadily, informing her that the life-support systems remained up, and so did SIPACUM. No spacefarer shut down those two survival systems. They were the heart, lungs, and brain of a spaceship.

Hopeless?

No! It's not hopeless! A week ago I didn't know what SIPACUM was. Now I can tear it apart and make minor repairs!

She could. And had. As had every member of the crew. Bogar had seen to that during their just completed run to Samanna. She had also brought *Windrammer* (in one functioning piece) home from Samanna.

Oh, true, Bogar had growled at her every parsec of the journey. It was she who had completed the flight, though. The snarly-crusty old spacefarer had never laid a finger on the controls.

And she had learned. Learned double the knowledge imparted by the injected brainboosts. So had her crew.

If two weeks isn't enough, then I find another captain to teach us!

She nodded with determination. She would have her ship and crew. It just might take longer than she had expected.

"Lizina," Chane called from behind her. "Hoku and I are going to the Hub Bar for lunch. Want to join us?"

Lizina swiveled around. Her First Mate and computrician stood by the door to the con-cabin. Chane's arm was about the young Terasak's waist. Hoku didn't seem to mind.

"I'll pass. Got a meeting onplanet." *Which you were supposed to attend with me*, she thought, but she left it unsaid.

Chane nodded. "See you when you get back, then."

Hoku's arm slipped about his waist as the two left Lizina alone within the con-cabin. She stared after them. A bittersweet smile touched the corners of her mouth.

Youth wins out once again!

Her smile widened to one of chagrin. Was it jealousy she felt—or relief?

A touch of both, old lady!

She laughed aloud. Her reaction to Chane's interest in Hoku was predictable—and silly. She had known the young man would eventually find another woman. If not the sexy little Terasak, then someone else.

Lizina already had someone else.

Chane and she had shared the same cabin during the Samanna run, but she had noticed his stolen gazes at Hoku, their smiles. Naturally Lizina had done nothing to intercede. When Dorjan arrived (she refused to consider "if" he arrived), things would be easier.

Lizina turned back to the con. She opened intership comm to Panishport Control. Two minutes later she was booked for a shuttle down in half an hour.

It wasn't much time. She'd make it. She had important matters to attend onplanet. Matters she had let slide during the run out to Samanna.

Under the watchful eye of Yemahl Huhleem, Lizina scanned the confidential reports. Then she went back to read them word for word. The attorney's investigators had been thorough.

"He appears financially sound." She keyed off the monitor and turned to Yemahl. "He might not be as easy to get at as I thought."

The senior member of Huhleem, Sudi, Yutu, Kwam & Progeny leaned back in his chair. He steepled his fingers over his chest. "Financial reports can be deceptive. The figures provide a portrait of a young man with a flair for investing. Making a quick return on his money, while stockpiling a tidy sum in steady, reliable securities."

"But?"

"But Thax Wilanu is a fool. His quick-kill investments are quite capable of doing exactly that. But to him." Yemahl smiled. "And his old, reliable securities . . . aren't."

Yemahl leaned forward. "Wilanu is bottom heavy with QTZ&R. Your husband had the foresight to sell his interest in the company eighteen months ago. Its foundations are crumbling, Lizina. Vardate Enterprises will drive them under when they announce their new, high energy-efficient converter."

Lizina knew nothing of the realm of business finance. Yemahl did. He had been one of Garold's top advisors.

"When will Vardate announce?" She had no idea what converter the attorney meant. Or what it was supposed to convert.

"They've been awaiting your approval. Garold owned forty-five per cent of Vardate's stock."

Which meant that she now owned the stock.

"And Thax's quick-kill investments?"

"Less clear cut, Lizina. But they have definite possibilities. That is, were one seeking to financially injure the man."

"Injure isn't good enough." Lizina stared at the lawyer. "I want him ruined—devastated. If I can take his last stell—legally—that's what I want."

Yemahl nodded. "Then the next question is, do you want him to know who is after him?"

"I want him to know that *someone* is draining him bone dry. But not who." *When the time comes, I'll be there to reveal the "who."* Casually she said, "Can you arrange that?"

Yemahl nodded. His facial expression was noncommittal, as though he dealt with such requests on a daily basis. A very, very cool man, Yemahl Huhleem, and just now Lizina was not minded to consider anyone's morality.

Perhaps he did hear and handle such requests regularly. Lizina didn't know. She didn't care, so long as he handled this for her—successfully.

"Our Thax Wilanu's quick-kill investments are in rather young firms." Yemahl had the monitor on again, studying the list of Thax's holdings. "I believe we can manipulate them readily. Perhaps make a handsome profit on the side."

"I don't care about the profit, Yemahl. Just Thax."

Yemahl glanced back to his client with an almost stern look. "When one can mix business—profitable business—with pleasure, it makes the transaction doubly pleasurable."

When she didn't smile, he returned his attention to the monitor. He hummed absently while he rubbed his chin.

"Yes. We purchase heavily here," (his fingers jabbed out) "let the market climb, then sell out quickly. Here we just sell."

He went on for ten minutes. A complete outline of the tactics he would employ against Thax. Lizina followed for a minute before electing to let him ramble on. She nodded occasionally. A charade to provide the impression that she understood all he was saying.

"And, of course, we'll need a diversion. Something to keep Wilanu's mind occupied while we maneuver." He flicked off the computer and swiveled back to Lizina. "An eviction would be nice to begin with. Payment records can be misplaced, you see. Even erased, without great difficulty."

Lizina nodded her approval. The more Yemahl said, the more she liked what she heard. It was not quite enough to make her smile, but she was getting there.

"Then a suit, perhaps two, should stir things up. We want him so worried he can't think straight."

"Suits. You mean lawsuits? What kind?" Her brow furrowed. "Will I be a party to them?"

"No no." Yemahl shook his head. "Rest assured, your name will be kept from any legal proceedings."

The attorney paused to stare past her. "And as to the nature of the suits, I haven't the slightest idea . . . at the moment. But there isn't a person in this galaxy who hasn't left himself open for a lawsuit. It's just a matter of investigation. It *will* take time."

"How long?"

"A month, perhaps two."

"Not good enough." Lizina pushed to the edge of her chair, and her eyes became as hard as the emeralds they resembled. "You have two weeks. Two weeks to complete everything. I want Thax in two weeks, Yemahl."

That brought his right eyebrow up. Yet that was his only comment. He simply rubbed his chin and hummed to himself.

"What about Mikk? Anything on him?"

"Very little." Yemahl's head tilted to the monitor. "Not even enough to enter a file. He's unmarried and without family. His only tangible asset is his cab. He owns it. He also has a decided taste for gambling. Although he controls it. Twice a year he places a series of heavy bets. Normally, he loses. Then he's not heard of until the next series of bets. Mostly on MercuryBall."

Money obtained from the sale of slaves, Lizina thought, but left the comment unspoken. Yemahl didn't know why she had disappeared from Panish so abruptly. She intended to keep it that way.

"Captain Kukis and his First Mate Degula appear to

be no more than the usual fare for those who travel the Tachyon Trail.'' The lawyer shrugged. ''They are ninety-nine per cent legitimate, but not above crossing to the other side of the law if there's a profit to be made.''

Lizina had experienced their crossing of that line first-hand. She needed no further explanation and didn't want any. She wanted *them*.

''They make a ten-planet circuit that brings them to Panish at least every four months. *Forerunner* is scheduled for Panish sometime this month. I couldn't pin down the arrival beyond that.''

''And Ganesa?''

''Nothing on the Reshan woman, her ship or crew. The Diamond Lady of Ganesa's Traveling Bakery Shoppe is apparently dead.'' Yemahl smiled even while he gazed into her eyes. His were bland.

A cold shiver punched up Lizina's spine at the lawyer's last comment. There was an indefinable something in his tone that said he knew more than he was saying.

Does he know about these past months? Or is he merely fishing—guessing?

Either way, he received no more than a noncommittal nod from his client as Lizina stood.

''Thax is the key,'' she said while she walked to the door to the office. ''He'll lead us to Mikk, Kukis, and Degula. And I want him in two weeks!''

With that, she redshifted. She had a ship and a crew to attend. And two weeks in which to master both.

11

"Why aren't they firing at the van?" Songan ducked back as a plasma bolt struck the side of the house in a pyrotechnic eruption that sprayed shards of synthestone.

"Kefira. Nav doesn't want to waste valuable property." Dorjan swung to the open door, squeezed his stopper twice, and leaped to the opposite side of the long hall.

In those brief seconds, he scanned the floodlit grounds. Five men in black jumpsuits lay prone out there in the grass. Two others lay crumpled and smoldering. Both were dead, killed by plasma bolts. Both represented a matter of luck rather than marksmanship on Songan's part.

Their deaths, however, had stopped the guards' advance on the front of the house.

As to where Nav and the remaining guards and two Lung Pao were, Dorjan wasn't certain. He was certain that if he and his companions didn't break free of the house soon, Nav would be breathing down their necks.

Songan shoved from the opposite wall and paused at the doorway just long enough to fire three rapid shots. In less than a heartbeat, he was pressed to the wall beside his captain.

A volley of shots answered his three. Sizzling plasma struck the door frame. Heat and bits of synthestone showered the two Harbians. Neither did damage.

"We're on the losing side of this standoff." Songan's

dark eyes rolled to his friend. "Nav's got time on his side. All he has to do is wait us out."

The crackling hiss of a plasma gun sounded behind them. Both men jerked around.

Varnalgeran Yuw stood at the end of the hall. A Dragon Panther lay smoldering at his feet.

"Nav decided to send in a scout," the man from Outreach called to his companions. "I think they're ready to try a rush from the flank."

"Hold down the fort here," Dorjan ordered his Mate, and he ran to Varn's side. "Let's see if we can change their minds, at least for a few minutes."

Dorjan pushed on ahead of the computrician. He ran toward the house's rear door.

Nav, the remaining Lung Pao, and the two missing guards were creeping toward the open back door.

Dorjan stepped into the doorway. He pointed (rather than aimed) his stopper at the nearest man; squeezed. As he jerked back out of the inevitable return, a scream tore from one of the black-jumpsuited men.

So did two plasma bolts. Each burned into the partially demolished wall just inside the house.

"You hit one." Varn was at his side, looking cool and unruffled. "In the arm. The swine's alive and he's still armed."

"Damn!" Dorjan cursed as he swung into the door and fired two additional shots.

Both went over the heads of guards and great cat, all of whom now lay in the grass. He didn't stand still long enough to see more, but jumped back to the Outie's side. A plasma burst rushed in after him. Only the opposite wall suffered.

"Captain . . . while Nav and his men are so conveniently positioned at the front and the rear of the house, it might be a good time to take a look around inside."

Varn stepped into the doorway and fired, then swung back to Dorjan. He looked up at the taller man. "There are windows all over this house, Dorjan. If the guards try a side attack, we won't be able to stop them.''

"Damn!'' Dorjan hadn't even considered the windows. "Hold them here. I'll be back as soon as I can!''

Leaping into the doorway, Dorjan squeezed off three quick shots and felt the hot breath of return fire as he retreated into the house. He opened the first door he came to. A closet.

"Great,'' he muttered and moved to the second.

The door opened into a study. His gaze passed over the wood paneling and the equally expensive hand-carved wooden furniture. A window, at least two meters long and a meter high drew his attention.

Crossing to it, he stared out at the jungle. For an instant he considered the possibility of making a run for the dense vegetation. No, he and his crew would never make it without being sighted. At least in the house they had cover.

With windows this exposed, he thought, it was only a matter of time until the house's relative security would be meaningless.

His glance shifted from side to side. A humorless smile tugged at his lips. The window was shuttered. He could just see the lip of plasteel above.

That meant there had to be a way of lowering that protective plate.

He found it atop the desk. A control panel, neatly labeled for every window in the house. Each was shuttered. Apparently Nav had anticipated a raid on his illegal TZ operation. The slimy toad had transformed his home into a fortress!

Two rows of toggles marched down the panel, and Dorjan smiled. They controlled locks on every door in the house! Not to mention the lighting—both indoors and out.

Indoors and out!

Dorjan's fingers trembled as he flicked the toggles to

shutter every window on the lower floor. Those on the second he left open. Those might, just might . . .

He tried to quell the thought. It wouldn't go away. As insane as it was, it was the one thing Nav wouldn't expect. No one would expect it. Dorjan stared at nothing, thinking.

First he had to check the upstairs rooms.

He returned to the front of the house at a run. He took the stairs three at a time and stepped over the three unconscious guards still lying where Yuw had dropped them. It was in the second bedroom he entered that he found what he wanted.

Outside, less than a meter from the room's window, a drainpipe was attached to the north side of the house. It was even considerate enough to be beyond the line of fire.

He found a button on the right side of the window sill and depressed it. The duraglas pane slid upward. Dorjan poked his head outside. He grinned. A rain gutter ran around the edge of the roof.

If the drain and gutter would support his weight, he was in business.

He pulled back into the house. There were no ifs about it. They *had* to support him. If they didn't, *Misfit* would be minus one winged captain.

At the head of the stairs, he climbed over the unconscious guards once again, then moved down to join his First Mate at the front door.

"What's upstairs?" Songan glanced at him questioningly.

"Our ticket out of here. *All* I have to do is make it to the roof!"

"Oh . . . that's all?"

Dorjan ignored his tattooed friend's doubtful look. Instead he called out to Edrek and Kefira.

"Can one of you wiggle up to the driver's seat?"

The affirmative reply was in Akil.

"Then do it," Dorjan said, and turned back to Songan. "No questions. In a few minutes it's going to get dark around here. When it does, make a break for the van. Varn will be on your heels. Don't wait for me. Just redshift the hell out of here."

Before Songan could reply, Dorjan was at the end of the hall. He stopped and glanced back to his friend. "Songan, if everything goes as I plan, I'll be waiting for you on the road to Deephole. I'm expecting a ride back into town. Don't forget to stop for me!"

"Don't forget to be there!" Songan called after him as he ran back to Varn.

Yuw stared at his captain if convinced he was as crazy as Dorjan felt. The Outie also agreed to follow his directions.

Exchanging his stopper for Varn's plasma pistol, Dorjan started back to the stairs in a run. He had exactly three minutes before the computrician abandoned his post and hit the light switches in the study. Three minutes!

Once more he took the stairs three at a time. Within the bedroom, he moved to the open window. He climbed half way out onto the ledge, grasped the drainpipe, and tugged.

It held. The metal didn't even groan. Now all it had to do was hold his full weight for the next minute.

Hands clamped to the pipe, he pulled himself from the window. His legs dropped beneath him, dangling.

The pipe groaned. Shuddered. Dorjan closed his eyes, feeling vulnerable as a two-year-old.

The drainpipe held.

Dorjan pulled his legs up and placed the soles of his boots flat against the synthestone wall. He released one hand and took a higher grip on the pipe. The left hand went above the right. Next came the feet. Right up one step, then the left.

Sem by sem, he wall-climbed toward the overhanging gutter. Right hand, left hand. Right foot, left foot. Three points in contact with the wall or pipe at all times. His heart was somewhere in the vicinity of his mouth, and he couldn't swallow.

Two meters up he crept before pausing. He eyed the gutter, then stretched out his right arm. His fingers curved over the gutter's lip. He tugged cautiously.

The gutter protested with a loud metallic creak. It also sagged visibly.

Dorjan glanced downward. Nav's neatly manicured lawn awaited him, seven meters below. It looked twice as far.

Not that far. If I land on my feet!

He lied to himself, and he knew it, somewhere back in there. Drop over three times the length of his body and land on his feet, and he might be wearing his knees up around his navel.

He sucked in a deep breath and pushed it from his lungs—and released the pipe with his left hand.

The gutter cried out in metallic anguish and buckled treacherously under his weight. A plasteel staple popped from the synthestone. Another. The gutter bent. It sagged, groaning, a full six sems. Then it stopped.

Feet and one arm adangle, Dorjan was wrenched from one side to the other. He flexed bioengineered muscles in his right hand. Unipolymer plasteel claws extended, made contact, cut into the gutter—and anchored him.

He swung back to face the house, and threw his left arm up. Claws and fingers locked to the gutter. He hung there for a long, uncertain second, waiting for the gutter to give again. It didn't.

Arms trained in the fighting arena of Harb pulled upward with a slow, steady pressure. The gutter was at chin level, then throat and then his chest. Dorjan rolled forward.

He paused, precariously balanced with only the gutter

for support, to release an overly held breath. Then he extracted the claws' grip on the sagging gutter.

Slowly, ever so slowly, he edged his arm upward along the roof. When it was fully extended, claws unsheathed again to dig into fiberplas shingles. They held.

He repeated the process with the left arm. Securely anchored to the roof, he pulled upward until only his booted feet hung over the edge of the roof. He allowed himself two deep breaths before he brought his legs under him so that he knelt on the slanted roof.

To both sides of his position came the crackling reports of plasma guns and the soft hum of stoppers. The sounds of the battle were reassuring. It meant that both Songan and Varn still held the doors to the house.

Dorjan gripped the bottom of the loose, black tunic he wore and yanked it over his head. Starting to toss the shirt off the roof, he stopped himself. He tucked it into the back of his pants instead.

It wouldn't do to have a winged man running around Deephole half-naked!

The half-naked part wasn't important. Concealing the gleaming wings that unfolded from his back was. Wings were hardly common attributes among Galactics. In fact Dorjan knew of only one man so equipped, and his name was Dorjan.

Slipping the plasma pistol from his belt, he knee-walked up to the roof's sharply slanted ridge. He peered to the front of the house. From this position the hovervan wasn't visible. Nav's guards, still prone in the grass, were. He mentally noted each. Once Yuw killed the lights, he would have no means of orienting himself to them.

His gaze lifted to the jungle that ringed the house. Fifty meters—if not more—stretched between him and the thick foliage and the security it offered. His wings would never make it.

The plasteel appendages attached to his back were not designed for true flight. With them fully extended, however, he could glide on them. From the roof, he could cover twenty-five meters—thirty, if he was lucky—before he touched the ground.

That was all he asked. The darkness and surprise would provide the edge he needed to make the jungle and the road. He hoped.

Dorjan edged closer toward the front of the house and crouched there on his haunches, chewing his lower lip. And he waited. Waited. His armpits prickled and his throat insisted that he needed a drink of water. Anything. He waited.

One moment floodlights bathed the lawn. The next, everything was shrouded in black.

Pushing to his feet, Dorjan ran to the front of the roof and threw himself into the air. His wings spread wide to caress the air. A human glider, he soared.

He pointed the plasma gun below, guesstimating the guards' position, and fired randomly. His finger pumped the trigger repeatedly while he did his best to empty the weapon's power-pack in the few seconds he had.

Screams and curses came from below. So did the whine of twin rotors. The hovervan moved! A grin spread across the soaring man's face. His crew had broken free of the house!

In the moonless darkness, Dorjan could only estimate his rate and speed of descent. He held himself arrow-straight and counted seconds. He listened but heard only the sound of rushing wind in his ears.

Unwilling to land face first in the grass, he pulled his legs under him and folded wings to back. The ground wasn't there.

Like a rock, he dropped—two meters—before striking solid earth. He grunted and rolled. Then he was on his feet, staggering one step, running straight ahead. He hardly slowed when he entered the jungle's protective vegetation. He angled to the left and the muddy road that led toward Deephole.

With the van's headlamps out, Edrek didn't see the man who stood at the edge of the road, waving his arms. The man was Edrek's captain. The hovervan shot by. Dorjan shouted and ran after it.

The whine of reversing rotors sliced the darkness. The van's rear door flew upward. Songan and Yuw waved their captain on while the van slowed. Both reached out, grabbed his arms, and hauled him inside.

"All safe and accounted for, Captain!" Varn said, and his grin practically connected his ears as the door closed behind Dorjan.

"For the moment, that is." Songan reached up to switch on a dome light. He tossed a clear packet filled with fine red powder.

Dorjan hefted the bag. It weighed at least a kilo.

"Tetrazombase?"

"There are two more just like it in this box." *Misfit*'s First Mate lifted a yellow plastic box from the floor of the van. He pointed to another box to the opposite side of the van. "Three more in there. Enough TZ to transform the residents of a small city into biological cyberunits."

Dorjan tossed the bag back into the box.

"This is why Nav's guards weren't firing on the van." Songan closed the box and dropped it beside its twin. "There's a large fortune here."

Dorjan stared at his friend. "I hope you're not thinking what I'm thinking."

"I don't think Mensah Nav is going to appreciate losing this." Songan sucked at his cheeks. "This is his planet. Everyone on it works for him."

It was. And everyone did.

Ginneh's sole Galactic settlement was Deephole, a company town that had been built to house the five thousand men and women who worked the cyprium mines. The rest of the planet was either jungle or ocean.

Dorjan turned and called to the front of the van, "Edrek, get the lights on! Then jam-cram for the shuttleport! Now!"

The youthful Lanatian did as told without so much as a questioning glance back at his captain.

Dorjan settled to the floor of the van. Nav would have one hell of a time outracing the van. Once they were at the shuttleport, there would be no stopping them!

12

There was a maxim among planetary policers: "A fugitive might be able to outrun my engine—but not my transmission."

Whether Mensah Nav had ever heard the rule of hot pursuit was not in question. The chief administrator of Ginneh's cyprium mines thoroughly grasped the concept, and that was sufficient.

He listened impatiently to his guards' unintelligible babblings about an aerial attack for exactly one minute before brushing them aside. Nav went directly to his study and flipped two rows of toggles. The house and grounds were once more lit.

Next he flicked on the phone and buttoned open a direct line to the two mines. The would-be hijackers who had robbed him of Kefira and a fortune in illegal tetrazombase were halfway to Deephole by now, and Mensah Nav wasn't an idiot. He knew he'd never catch them by giving chase.

But he could outrun them and their stolen red van. They would never make it offplanet. Not with all of Deephole after them! And Mensah Nav had the populace of Ginneh's sole settlement at his beck and call.

The two mine foremen he spoke with had no questions about his explicit instructions. The four men and the golden-furred alien woman were to be captured—alive or dead.

Nav also grasped a concept police had made use of for millennia; eons before humankind dreamt of leaping from the planet they now called Homeworld into the limitless expanse of space. The simple concept was that loyalty or any other moral stricture could and did move individuals to action—occasionally.

Gold, however, was far more predictable.

Nav offered ten kilostells for the van and its contents, intact. Two kilostells for each of the four thieves and the kidnapped Akil. The latter he also preferred intact. After all, she was a rarity. *Une type*; a one-of-a kind item.

The four men he preferred . . . dead.

Five minutes after Nav hung up, half of Deephole knew of the reward. Twenty-five hundred men and women could already feel the weight of those promised interstellar credits in their pockets.

"Kill the lights!" Dorjan ordered as Edrek rounded a sharp bend in the muddy road. "Hover this thing!"

Edrek did as told. He turned back to his captain. "What's wrong?"

Dorjan shook his head, peering into the night ahead. He couldn't put a finger on it, but something was wrong, and he knew it.

"Songan, Varn, take a look."

They scooted over beside their captain to stare through the van's windscreen. Ahead lay Deephole. Dorjan's own gaze traced and retraced the half-klom dirt strip that was jokingly referred to as Main Street. (The crude road was Deephole's only street.)

Buildings, none over three stories high, lined each side of the muddy strip that ran from north to south. Every Galactic-made structure onplanet (with the exception of Nav's home) was on Main Street. The road dead-ended to the north. There lay the shuttleport.

To the east and west was a soft glow of lights—the cyprium mines.

"I don't notice anything," Yuw said from Dorjan's right. "Deephole looks about as busy—or lazy as usual, depending on your point of view."

Varn was right. For the daytime.

But dawn was at least an hour and a half away. There were too many people on Main Street for this hour. Dorjan was sure of that: he and Songan had made the trek back from Nav's house in the predawn hours every day for a week.

"There's too many lights on and too many people." Songan sank back to the floor. "Nav has prepared a welcoming committee for us. The whole town's turned out!"

Dorjan's head nodded without his knowledge while his gaze ran down the half-klom of Main Street. To attempt a straight run for the shuttleport would be suicide. Even with the hovervan gunned to full speed they *might* make a quarter klom. Stoppers would be useless against the van. The trouble was that this was a mining planet. Explosives and plasma guns were readily available.

It wouldn't take an expert marksman or even luck to knock out the van. A plasma gun in the hands of a child would do the trick. All it had to do was point and keep squeezing the trigger. Main Street was too narrow for the shots to miss for long.

"Suggestions?" Dorjan glanced at Songan and Yuw.

It was Kefira who spoke. "Give me and the TZ back to Nav. The four of you might be able to make it through the town unnoticed. But there is no way to disguise my appearance."

"No!" Edrek's head snapped around to the Akil. His arms shot out, hands firmly clamping atop her shoulders to let her know he would never allow such a ridiculous scheme.

Three voices from the rear of the van echoed his cry of dismay.

Kefira was right, Dorjan realized. Even in her HOME-spun jumpsuit, the silky golden down of her face and the white-gold of her shoulder-length hair were unmistakably alien.

Ginneh was a Galactic planet. Here, as on all Galactic worlds, skin pigmentation lighter than golden-brown was more than just a rarity; it was unheard of.

The same was true of hair. Black and dark brown were the rule, despite the wide use of dyes and exotic wigs.

When the vast majority of the peoples of Homeworld-Urth had seized the planet and gone into space as Galactics, they had done a thorough job of destroying the old ruling minority and overwhelming its genetic lesser pigmentation. Even Universal Edutapes did not mention the word "Caucasian."

"Here. This might help."

Varnalgeran Yuw sighed loudly and shrugged. With an embarrassed glance at his companions, he took off his wide-brimmed Wayne and passed it forward to Kefira.

"Stuff as much of that lovely hair as you can under this." He watched her gather the white-gold cascade and pile it atop her head before donning the Wayne. "Now pull the brim low. And up with your collar."

Dorjan grinned. That great big hat was perfect! Kefira's delicate face and those oh-so round gold-flecked eyes were completely shadowed by the brim. The raised collar hid the sleek gold down of her neck.

"Edrek, yank off the feathers and the beads! If Kefira keeps her hands in her pockets, it just might work." Songan leaned forward, his gaze critically appraising the Akil's altered appearance.

"Hey!" Varn's arm shot out to stop his crewmate's assault. He reacted far too slowly.

Edrek gave one quick tug and the bead-and-feathers hatband tore free. Now Varn's Wayne resembled one of the thousand wide-brimmed hats worn by Ginnehers to shade them from the jungle sun.

"No appreciation for beauty," Varn said with a genuine moan of pain.

"If we make it offplanet, I'll buy you one twice as gaudy." Songan looked at his Outie friend. "And a new Wayne thrown in to boot."

"No! And boots!" Varn amended.

"I'll buy the damned boots, if you can get us offplanet." Dorjan's gaze returned to Deephole and the half-klom of Main Street that stretched before them. "Any suggestions as to how the hell we're going to get through that?"

"Throw in a couple of shirts and pairs of pants—of my choosing—and I just might." Varn grinned widely and winked at his captain.

"Damn your Outie ass—you can have a whole sisterslicing wardrobe if you can get us offplanet!"

"An offer no Outie could refuse." Yuw paused and ran a hand through thinning hair. "But the best I might be able to do is have a shuttle ready and waiting at the port. Can't fly one of those things, you know."

"Varn, this isn't . . ." *the time for jokes*, Dorjan had meant to say. Only the somber look on his computrician's face told him Yuw was not joking.

"You've got something in mind?"

"An idea."

"Let's hear it," Songan joined in.

"You don't want to hear it," Yuw assured them, and took a deep breath. "But if you give me a shot at it, I think I can walk you right down the middle of Main Street without anyone batting an eye."

No comment greeted his dramatic pause. "I'll need some help. Edrek, has this thing got an auto control?"

Edrek glanced at the con. "Yes, but . . ."

"No buts. We haven't time. It'll be light soon. If we intend to get offplanet it has to be before dawn."

Varn paused again. "The first thing we've got to do is get this van off the road and into the brush. Nav and his men are going to be coming this way any time now. After that, it'll be up to the captain and me."

"Me?" Dorjan stared at him.

"I said I'd need help," Varnalgeran Yuw said, and shrugged.

As Yuw had predicted, several of Deephole's residents had positioned themselves in the jungle on either side of town. Skirting Main Street to reach the shuttleport was an obvious route for five fugitives.

Perhaps so obvious that no one expected them to try the jungle.

The two men Dorjan and Varn came upon were joking and passing a stick of Mildhigh between them. Both dropped without a sound. Stoppers on the modified second setting provided the password beyond the jungle checkpoint.

Dorjan paused only to strip the men of their weapons—two plasma pistols—and he and Yuw moved on.

A four-person floater and a bike shot by on the road.

Songan relaxed, unaware that his body had tensed so at the approach of the vehicles. He turned to Edrek and Kefira. Both looked as nervous as he felt.

He didn't like being left here. He damn sure didn't like the wait. He'd rather be out there in the predawn morning with Dorjan and Yuw.

"Should I move the van back onto the road?" Edrek's hands reached for the controls.

"Not yet. There might be more of Nav's men coming." Songan silently cursed the thick foliage about the van. He couldn't see Deephole from their position. "Or Nav might send someone out to backtrack when he learns we haven't entered town yet. We'll follow Varn's plan."

Edrek grunted. His inarticulate reply said he disliked the waiting as much as his respected friend.

"It's crazy!" Edrek slammed a fist against the van's door. "There's no way we'll be able to just walk into Deephole without someone noticing! Varn didn't make any sense."

"Our Outie friend isn't known for making sense. He sure does have a knack for getting the job done, though."

Songan wished he felt as certain as his voice sounded.

In twenty minutes, he and his companions were to abandon the van and walk into Deephole. They were to make no attempt to conceal their presence. Simply walk into the mining town and head directly for the shuttleport, that was the plan. Or "plan."

Edrek was right. It didn't make sense. Had Songan been a believer in either Musla or Booda, he would have prayed. Like his captain, he was a Taoist.

What will be, will be.

The trouble with that philosophy was that it was mighty short on comfort.

Dorjan crouched (at a safe distance) behind the bore of a needle-spine tree. Twenty meters beyond his position, the jungle had been cleared. At the center stood two high-rising conveyer belts and several less-than-sturdy-appearing buildings. The structures surrounded the entrance to the cyprium mine to the east of Deephole.

Dorjan's objective lay at the edge of the clearing: a small corrugated plasteel building. DANGER EXPLOSIVES was stencilled on its single locked door in bright red letters.

The master of *Misfit* did not question how Varn knew

about the shed. That it was exactly where he said was
enough.

Perhaps this isn't as crazy as it sounded, he thought,
in an attempt to quell his entirely natural doubts about
Yuw's scheme.

The hint of a smile touched the corners of his mouth
as he moved from the jungle's vegetation to the shed.
His right forefinger (vibe-knife extended) sheared the
lock in seconds.

Inside, he located the case of incendiaries right where
the Outie said that they would be. Even the case's lid
was ajar as Varnalgeran had described.

Stuffing five of the grenade-sized explosives into his
shirt, Dorjan left the shack and slipped back into the
rain forest. He had fifteen minutes to get back to Deephole
and position himself.

Varnalgeran Yuw's stopper was set on Three. He
held it to the controller's temple. His plasma gun was
trained on the shuttleport's three firemen.

What remained of the fourth man lay on the floor. He
had made the mistake of believing he could take the
overweight Outie off guard. Yuw's stopper had corrected the fool's error.

"Stir it well."

Varn's eyes shifted to the controller and the flo-point
pen he used to stir the four paper cups of water. The
man nodded nervously and swirled the pen with in-
creased vigor.

"Now, drink one and pass the others to your friends."

From the corner of an eye, the Outie watched the
man pick up the first plass. He downed its watery
contents in one hard-swallowed gulp.

"It's not poison!" Varn smiled humorlessly. "Give
your friends theirs. Consider yourselves lucky. You're
about to lose eight hours of your lives, and after that

you'll be yourselves again. And you *will* be alive, which is more than can be said for *him*!''

The muzzle of the plasma gun dipped to the seared human carcass on the floor just for an instant. The gesture was understood. The three men downed the TZ-laced water the controller handed them.

Yuw motioned for the standing man to take the empty seat beside the three. He did. All four stared at the Outie and his guns as though expecting to die in the next instant.

They wouldn't. It was just that in five minutes they would be biological robots that moved at Yuw's command. With their help—and the three bags of tetrozombase Varn carried inside his shirt—*Misfit*'s crew just might make it to the shuttle that sat on the runway, ready and waiting.

The Outie's eyes inspected the small room. Beyond the card table (a lucky break that, finding the five engrossed in a WinTag game!—easier than having to round them up) was the shuttleport's comm console.

Varn stepped toward the unit, keeping his pistols leveled on the four. He had a very important message to send before he attended to the two firetrucks outside.

Deephole's lone hotel was the Rich Vein. Three stories of natural rock and wood, it hulked on the east side of Main Street. If there was a center point to the half-klom stretch of buildings, it was the Rich Vein.

Dorjan approached the hotel from the rear. Unseen, he faded out of the jungle and into Rich Vein's rear entrance. He paused inside, listening. The hotel was silent.

Left arm cradling the heavy incendiaries tucked into his shirt, he moved down a long hall toward the hotel's lobby. He paused at the end of the corridor and peered around the corner.

The lobby was empty. Even the clerk was missing from his usual position behind the registration desk.

Dorjan didn't question his fortune. From the voices that came from outside he realized that Deephole's residents were gathered along the street to await the arrival of the thieves who had struck Nav's home. Stopper gripped in right hand, he ran across the lobby. He passed the elevator and moved up the less-used stairs.

On the third floor, he located a door to the roof. Once more his vibe-knife fingernail provided a key to the lock. Up a short flight of stairs and he stood on the hotel's roof.

In a half-crouch he crossed to the front of the building. Squatting, he extracted the incendiaries from his shirt—carefully. He laid each of the five before him on the flat roof. When the time came he need only reach down, thumb-flip the timer, and toss. Five times.

He glanced to the left. The flat roofs of the buildings running northward toward the shuttleport offered an unobstructed egress for a winged man. He smiled. He would need that way out.

Laying the stopper beside the explosives, Dorjan pulled the plasma pistol from his belt and eased forward to gaze down at Main Street. Across the muddy road, he saw Nav and two of his guards. Surrounding the three was a crowd of at least fifty miners.

Dorjan's smile grew to a grin. Varn couldn't have asked for better positioning!

His gaze shifted to the south and the road that disappeared into the jungle darkness. In five minutes a red hovervan would shoot from that blackness to barrel down Main Street. With its appearance all hell would break loose.

Until then, Dorjan simply waited.

*   *   *

Varnalgeran Yuw held his breath while he ripped open the last bag of TZ and dumped it into the tank of water. Screwing the cap back onto the wide mouth, he jumped down.

He sucked in a lungful of air while he eyed the two hovertrucks—and smiled. Both were pump trucks (complete with bellying tanks of water) used for shuttleport fire control. The two engines also doubled as Deephole's fire fighting force.

This morning the trucks' self-contained water supply also carried three kilos of tetrazombase.

Varn remembered Songan's word: *Enough TZ to transform the residents of a small town into biological cyberunits.* Which, with Theba's "smiling" grace, was exactly what he intended to do.

He walked to the cab of the first truck and for the third time, repeated his instructions to the two drugged men within. He did the same for the two inside the second truck.

Lastly, he climbed into a floater that stood behind the two pump trucks. And he waited for the wail of the alarms.

Edrek punched the auto-control button on the console and jumped from the open door of the hovervan. Songan and Kefira, face shadowed by the wide-brimmed Wayne, ran to his side. The three watched the van trundle northward along the road toward Deephole.

"Let's move. The moment that van rolls onto Main Street, Deephole is going to come apart at the seams." Songan urged his companions after the van.

The waiting was over. Now it was a matter of timing.

Dorjan saw the van first. A second later, shouts below told him that Deephole's residents had noted its approach. From the jungle to each side of the road, miners abandoned their concealment and chased after the mud-splattered vehicle.

Now, Songan. Move it! Use the confusion!

Even as he silently urged his companions on, Dorjan raised his plasma gun and sighted on the approaching van, which he very well knew was driverless. He aimed not at the vehicle's blunted front, but toward the rear and the fuel tank located there.

From both sides of Main Street, miners ran out in front of the van. Pistols were raised. Not a one was used. Male and female alike, the miners scattered, running, slipping in the mud, when the hovervan did not slow.

Can they see it's driverless?

Dorjan never received an answer to his silent question. It didn't matter. What did matter was that the van was now almost directly below him.

His finger tightened around the trigger of the plasma pistol. And squeezed.

Tongues of red and yellow shot from the exploding van, licking upward into the predawn sky. Thunder rolled in an ear-shattering chorus. Heat, a concussion wall of searing heat, blasted through the street. Predawn became false dawn.

There was one frozen moment of shock and confusion before every man and woman on Main Street ran toward the burning vehicle. Black smoke boiled up like grease.

Songan, Edrek, and Kefira (hands now tucked in her pockets) ran, too. Edrek did likewise.

No one noticed the three who trotted into town from the jungle road. The sky-licking tongues of flames held the attention of every Ginneher in Deephole.

Dorjan grabbed the first incendiary from the roof. Thumbing the arming switch, he lobbed his missile in a high arc. The explosive sailed through the darkness toward the roof of the building directly across from the hotel.

Before it landed, he had tossed a second incendiary to the roof of the building to his right. A third was flying across the street, angled to leftward, before the first exploded in an actinic glare of white.

By the time the third went off, Dorjan had thrown the remaining two firebombs downward into the smoldering wreckage of the van.

His gaze scanned the miners below. He smiled. He could pick out Yarn's forlornly deplumed and debeaded Wayne moving through the crowd. No one heeded the alien woman beneath the hat. No one paid attention to the two men walking beside her. All eyes stared at the four fires that had abruptly erupted in their town.

Gathering his stopper from the roof, Dorjan ran back from the front of the hotel. He yanked off his tunic and tossed it aside. If Deephole's residents hadn't noticed the Akil woman below, they wouldn't notice a winged man gliding from rooftop to rooftop on his way to the shuttleport.

The two pumper trucks rolled from the shuttleport at the first wail of the fire alarms. Behind them (at a safe distance) followed an Outie-driven floater car.

Within a minute the two firetrucks pulled before the blazing wreckage of a van that once had been red. The four men in the cabs piled out to attach hoses to the water tanks.

Several car lengths from the trucks' position, Yuw braked his floater. A pleased smile twitched his lips as he watched the rather awkward attempt to direct the spray of water onto the van and the three buildings ablaze on each side of the street.

The crowd that gathered to watch the flames was soaked. Drenched. Men and women scattered across the muddy street. They sputtered and coughed, trying to clear their mouths of the half-swallowed deluge.

It appeared to be an accident. It wasn't. Merely an order implanted into four drug-controlled minds.

Yuw's smile widened to a self-satisfied grin. There was a certain poetic justice in the scene. A planet that was responsible for the production of tetrazombase would within five minutes be under the control of that drug (and would remain that way for a maximum of eight hours). And if Yuw was anything, he was poetic. He was, after all, an Outie.

One of the misdirected spouts of water was swung onto the burning van. The other gushed onto one of the three burning buildings. By then, the man from Outreach no longer watched the fire-fighting scene. He backed the car down the street toward the shuttleport.

Three passengers, who had slipped from the crowd during the confusion, grinned at him from the back seat.

Dorjan met his crew at the gates as Yuw wheeled into the shuttleport. A door swung upward and the winged man climbed in beside the Outreacher. Yuw's foot pressed the throttle to the floor. The floater moved out onto the runway and the shuttle that awaited them.

"Captain, I'm afraid I didn't foresee every problem in our escape." Varn looked at Dorjan sheepishly. He tilted his head to the back seat.

Dorjan turned to congratulate his three companions on the way they had handled themselves. His lower jaw dropped. All three were soaking wet.

Songan shrugged and grinned. "TZ is absorbed by the skin. It's not as fast acting as when taken internally or injected. But in about thirty minutes, you're going to have three human robots on your hands. I suggest you get us to *Misfit* as quickly as possible."

Dorjan shot his computrician a look. Varn's shoulders slumped forward.

"Sorry, Captain." The Outie braked beside the shuttle. "I just wasn't thinking."

"Better start thinking in double time," Dorjan said as he stepped from the car and waved his crew into the waiting craft. "For the next eight hours you're going to have to be *Misfit*'s Mate *and* computrician!"

Inside the ship, Songan directed Yuw to the co-pilot's seat. "I don't trust myself to last long enough to make rendezvous. Dorjan won't have much use for a Mate gone frag on TZ."

Yuw nodded reluctantly and took the co-pilot's place. By the time he strapped himself in, Dorjan had ignited the thrusting rockets. The shuttle hurtled down the runway into the face of Ginneh's rising sun.

There was a moment of physical and mental disorientation. A sickening rush of nausea. In the next instant, all was normal. Thus *Misfit,* transformed atom for atom into faster-than-light tachyons, leaped into "subspace."

Dorjan swiveled to his computrician. "Better check on Songan, Edrek, and Kefira. *Misfit*'s never carried anyone zapped on TZ before, let alone half its crew!"

More than a little distraught and showing it, Varn rose and headed for the con-cabin's door. His gaze never met Dorjan's.

"By the way, Varn. I forgot to mention that was one hell of a miracle you performed in Deephole. Remind me the next time we're on a civilized planet that I owe you *two* new wardrobes."

The overweight Outie glanced back at his captain. A wide grin split his face. "Of my choosing?"

Dorjan laughed. "Booda help our eyes—but yes, of your choosing!"

Yuw winked and redshifted to check on his three drugged crewmates.

Dorjan swiveled back to the con. He didn't like the idea of traveling the Tachyon Trail with half his crew incapacitated. But they *were* in subspace. And they *were* alive.

And most importantly, they were on their way to HOME.

13

Thax Wilanu stood in the street—Kahmloh Avenue, an exclusive residential district for Harmony's rich. Around him were piled (in shocking disorder) his possessions.

He stared at the building superintendent in total disbelief. The veins of his neck thickened and pushed outward with each word Thax uttered. His face was scarlet with anger. He couldn't accept that this had happened. Not to *him*! "You bastard! You can't be serious! I've never missed my rent once in the three years I've lived here!"

"That's not what the owners say." The fat little man held up a computer printout. "Their accounts show you haven't paid in three months. No stells—no penthouse!"

The superintendent pivoted and moved at a rapid waddle back toward the apartment building. He grumbled to himself. His wife had assured him that managing apartments at this classy address would be a cushiony job. Oh sure. It was like all the other buildings he had supered. No hot water. No air-con. No heat. And now evictions for no-pay!

"You bug! You can't walk away from me like that! Not while I'm still talking to you!"

Thax's ego could not endure the insult of having the mushy-faced man turn his back on him. With three running steps, he was on the superintendent. He grabbed him by the arm and jerked him around. Thax's right fist flew forward. Its flight was stopped abruptly by the man's swinish nose.

The super went down, arms and legs flaying the air. He careened across the slidewalk and into a very solid and unyielding guard rail post.

He did not rise. He lay quite still, eyes closed.

The incident probably would have ended there, had not a policer been among the small crowd of onlookers who had gathered at the sound of angry voices.

Soon Thax was arrested (assault and battery, creating a public disturbance, and assault on an officer of the law—undoubtedly his worst offense, but the policer had not been such easy prey as the unconscious superintendent). His wrists were field-cuffed and he was hastened to the local CP via a summoned squad car.

The building superintendent was meanwhile hurriedly conveyed to the emergency room of a nearby hospital. He was duly treated for a broken nose and minor concussion. A young intern—putting in his first day in ER—ordered the man kept overnight for observation. The injuries were minor, but he was overly cautious. A lawsuit could ruin a physician just getting started.

Thax remained behind bars for five hours. He'd have been released sooner, but his attorney was off-pager at a MercuryBall tourney. He spent the night in a local hotel considerably removed from his possessions, which were in a storage warehouse. He slept soundly, assured by his attorney that the rent matter would be cleared up and his penthouse back the next day.

Yemahl Huhleem finished keying the coded message to *Windrammer*. Lizina Harith would be pleased with the day's results. He was.

He had sold a large block of Biamin Limited shares at noon. By closing, the stock had plunged from five stells a share to one twentieth that. The transaction had little bearing on the overall market. Biamin was, after all, a small electronics firm.

Thax Wilanu, however, had lost twenty thousand stells in the maneuver. Unfortunately he wouldn't know that until morning, since his broker hadn't been able to contact him while he had been locked behind bars.

Yemahl smiled. He could imagine Wilanu's expression in the morning. The thought of his misery warmed Huhleem's heart.

The attorney wasn't certain what this Wilanu had done to Lizina Harith. He could guess, and did. It wasn't hard to put two and two together. How else would such a fine woman as the widow of Garold Harith know of Ganesa and her space traveling whorehouse—unless Lizina had been kidnapped and sold to the woman!

Yemahl wasn't against slavery *per se*. He just didn't like to see his clients mistreated. Especially those who were as rich and lovely as Lizina Harith.

For an instant a very erotic fantasy flitted through Yemahl's mind. Within it was a very naked—except for knee-length black boots—Lizina. And an equally nude Yemahl Huhleem; a very willing slave to the young woman's every desire.

Old fool!

Yemahl edged the enticing vision aside. Lizina had never given him more than a strictly attorney-client look.

Still, Musla might be smiling on him. Hadn't Thax Wilanu dropped the grounds for a very solid lawsuit into his lap? The building superintendent was adamant about wanting to file—especially after Yemahl explained that an unknown benefactor was willing to assume all legal expenses.

Perhaps when he demonstrated to Lizina how capable he was, she would see him in a new light. She *had* married Garold Harith. And no one could have described Garold as a handsome man; only a rich one.

Again, Yemahl admitted that he was probably just daydreaming. Still, he saw no harm in such delicious daydreams.

Very unladylike sweat beaded Lizina's forehead. It definitely could not be called perspiration. Large, wet rings radiating from her armpits had completely ruined the Kelly green blouse she wore. It was tied in a loose knot beneath her breasts so that it exposed the silky expanse of her flat midriff. It would not, she realized, be flat much longer.

She noticed neither. Nor was she aware of her provocative attire.

For the past two hours her attention had been focused solely on the con. *Windrammer* was under attack. Lizina's adversary was none less than the infamous Captain Corundum.

In that two hours, she had successfully eluded two head-on volleys and three seeker-torps. She had also managed to keep her prow facing the pirate, no matter how serpentine his maneuvering.

Inexperienced or not, she grasped the importance of not exposing the vulnerable broadside of her ship to Corundum's DS. Not if she wished to keep ship, crew, and her own life.

"Boldua," she called over intraship comm, "I think he's tracking our DS with scan-sensors. I'm going to shove *Windrammer* to see-oh-one-seven. When we peak, DS will go manual. Try to sneak a beam to his midship!"

"Particle beamer at maneuver peak," her DS officer acknowledged.

"Initiate offensive maneuver in five," she said, down-counting five seconds.

Lizina's fingers jabbed at the console. The ship's sub-light drive kicked in. Two gees of instantaneous acceleration pushed her into her seat's cushioning. A "+" on the monitor swung upward to grid square C-017.

The "–" representing Corundum's ship was . . .

"Chane! Where's the bastard!" Lizina couldn't find the pirate's ship.

"I've lost him!" Chane's voice was two octaves higher than normal. Panicked. "Sensors aren't scanning him."

"SIPACUM reads redshift." This from Hoku the Terasak computrician. "He's gone subspace."

"Boldua, stow the particle beamer. Track manually at a full three hundred and sixty global!" Lizina called to her DS officer. Hurriedly she swung *Windrammer* about . . . as hurriedly as its velocity allowed.

It didn't make sense for the pirate to vanish so suddenly. He had no reason to make a run for it. Why had he disappeared? Furthermore and more importantly— where?

"Chane, keep sensors up and scanning." Lizina read the arrays and mini-displays. Still nothing. "Hoku! Anything from SIPACUM?"

The young Terasak's head started to turn. Half around to Lizina, it jerked back to SIPACUM. "Booda! He's off port side! And he's fired three torps!"

"How!" Panic-stricken, Lizina's gaze swept the con, seeking—*anything*!

"Bang!" A throaty growl boomed over the intraship comm. *"You're dead!"*

"Bastard!" Lizina said, but under her breath.

She sank back into her chair. She was drained— mentally and physically—from the two-hour ordeal.

And she had lost the simulated duel.

Her ship was now random atoms scattered across the galaxy. And she and her crew were dead.

"Set a course to Panishport," Bogar's voice ordered

from the grille. "We've got cargo to load before the
Lanatia run. I'll be up in a moment."

Shakily, Lizina's hands returned to the console. She
punched in the coordinates Hoku fed her from SIPACUM.
Windrammer's drive ignited for a three-minute burn.

With the ship under power, Lizina collapsed back
into her chair once more. She looked apologetically at
Hoku and turned the same look on Chane.

"Don't worry about it." Chane's voice was steeped
in sympathy. "It was only a game, Lizina—a simula-
tion. You lasted two hours! Against Corundum!"

"Two hours! Booda's miraculous cubes, boy!"

The three at the con twisted around. Bogar stood in
the cabin doorway. None of them had heard the hatch
hiss open.

"Two hours doesn't mean a thing. If you get yourself
killed, how long it takes doesn't win any prizes. Dead
is dead!" Bogar's glare shifted from one to the other of
the three of them. "And your Captain just got you
killed!"

He paused for a breath before resuming his tirade.
"Don't think for a minute my preprogrammed cassette
was anything like meeting the real Captain Corundum!
If *he* ever crosses your trail, have the common sense to
let the man board and take what he wants. Consider
yourselves lucky if he leaves you with your lives!"

"How did he disappear off the sensor screens?"
Lizina's downcast eyes rose to her burly mentor.

"Damned if I know!" Bogar's granite-hard features
seemed to soften for an instant. "He pulled the same
stunt some ten years ago. Still don't know how he
managed it. Maybe you'll find out next time we run the
cassette!"

The next time!

Lizina already dreaded the occasion.

*   *   *

"A stell a share?" Thax repeated the broker's price quotation in disbelief. "You must be joking! That stock was worth twenty a share when the market opened this morning!" His voice climbed the scale toward hysteria and Thax didn't notice.

"That was before Vardate's announcement. Since then the bottom's dropped out from under QTZ&R. I tried to call you earlier, but couldn't reach you." The man on the phone screen looked as if he had just returned from a funeral—his own.

Thax felt the same way.

"I was unavoidably detained by other matters." Thax cursed the apartment superintendent silently in language quite unbecoming a member of Panish's upper class. The bastard was suing him for five hundred kilostells. For a broken nose and a bump on the head! Thax had been stuck in a preliminary hearing when the broker had tried to contact him.

"Thax, I advise you to sell now while I've got a buyer on the line," his broker told him, not quite coldly. "I know your losses will be heavy. But at least you'll come away with something."

"No!" Thax shook his head with a jerk. "QTZ&R is too old a firm to collapse. Somebody's just trying to shake things up and make a killing by buying while everyone else is panicked. I'll stick with my stock. The price will rise again."

"Thax, I don't believe you understand the situation. Vardate's converter has made every piece of equipment QTZ&R manufactures obsolete. The company won't stand."

"You heard me. I won't sell this low! I can't afford to. Three-quarters of everything I have is tied to QTZ&R!"

"You can't afford not to . . ."

Thax buttoned off the phone. He was unwilling to

listen to more. *A stell a share!* Did that moron think he'd gone frag?

Thax Wilanu ran both his hands through neatly trimmed black hair. His gaze rose to stare at a hotel wall.

Flaining hell! The whole damn galaxy is after me!

A cold shudder ran up his spine. He pushed the errant thought aside. It couldn't be. He was just frightened. He knew people—mingled with people with that type of power. He had gone out of his way to keep his nose clean around them. No one could be after him. *No! Not me!*

Nobody he knew would destroy QTZ&R simply to get at him!

Hoku's dark eyes studied Chane. "Do you love her?"

Chane glanced away. Two weeks ago he would not have hesitated in giving an unreserved "yes" to the question. Now, he wasn't certain. Now there was Hoku.

"I understand if you do." Hoku's voice was soft. "Our captain is very beautiful. Any man would find her desirable. It would be difficult to turn from her bed."

Chane rolled to his side to face the young woman. His right hand moved under the sheet. It glided over the gentle swell of Hoku's stomach, easing ever upward to caress the delicate perfection of her breasts.

Small when compared to Lizina's more assertive warheads, Hoku's were every bit as sensitive. He felt the excited tremors that coursed through her diminutive body. Awakened and fired by the brushing strokes of his fingertips, she began to squirm.

The beautiful Terasak's fingers were doing some awakening of their own. His slicer was coming to attention once again. He was very nearly astonished; mere minutes had passed since it had been so expertly sated.

"Do you love her?" Hoku asked again.

"Yes . . . but it's not like the way I feel for you," Chane said. He knew he was no longer sure of the feelings he held for Lizina. "It's a . . . loyalty. The love one feels for a member of one's family."

"On Terasaki that is called incest."

There was no malice in Hoku's voice, but that made her words sting all the more. Chane winced inwardly.

"I'm saying it wrong. Everything is jumbled in my head. I love Lizina. But I *love* you, Hoku. Do you understand?"

Long jet lashes veiled her eyes, and she nodded. It was a "yes" that meant "no." The answer only compounded the guilt Chane felt for sharing Lizina's bed while he stole time to be with Hoku.

His fingertips abandoned the enticing mounds of Hoku's warheads to trace the gentle curve of her mouth. He leaned to her and his lips lightly touched hers.

"I do love you, Hoku."

"I know." Her gaze rose to him once again. Her dark eyes were deep and mesmerizing. "You serve our Captain. And I serve you. It is all I want. To serve you."

She snuggled closer. Her lips tauntingly teased at his neck, then worked leisurely downward. A delicious shudder coursed through every cell of his body when those delicate lips opened to encompass the hard shaft of his slicer.

Thoughts of Lizina—of guilt—evaporated. Chane's attention focused on this exciting golden woman and the magic she wove with lips and tongue. What Hoku lacked in experience, she more than adequately made up for in her sheer, unashamed enthusiasm for the task she undertook.

Squirming, shuddering, Chane reached for her head.

It had been a busy week. Mikk had fully intended to make the insurance payment; he had forgotten. The cab was his. And it was a steady source of income . . . his livelihood. He'd been stupid. It had been an oversight.

The damned accident had been such a *minor* one! Nobody had been injured. His taxi required no more than a few dents pounded from the rotor skirts and a touch-up paint job.

The other car, however, was a Comet Q90-T. The price for a strip of chrome (*real* chrome) on one of those babies ran in double kilostell figures.

Mikk hadn't damaged a strip of chrome.

His cab had swiped the comet from nose to stern. Gouging a deep trough of twisted metal along the car's length. In the process, he shattered the bubble dome and mangled the Comet's rotors (*four*, rather than the standard two).

The owner had, of course, sued the moment he had learned of Mikk's expired liability insurance. The court had impounded Mikk's credaccounts and slapped an injunction on him that prohibited the use of the cab until the case was adjudicated.

At the moment, Mikk had fifty stells in his pocket. With luck, he could stretch them until the end of the week.

And after that? What do I do then?

He wasn't certain. He was a cab driver. It was all he knew. And now . . . no company would give him the time of day with a lawsuit hanging over his head.

Yemahl Huhleem read over the end-of-the-day reports. He hummed and rubbed at his chin. A few snags had developed in the Tarmos case that would require his personal attention.

A damned nuisance, that. He should have allowed his youngest son to run off and become a spacefarer as the boy had wanted when he was in his teens. Yemahl's son had just celebrated his thirtieth birthday and still displayed no inkling of grasping what it meant to be a lawyer.

On the other hand, the Harith *arrangements* were coming along quite nicely.

He made a mental note to give a bonus to the investigator who had uncovered Mikk's expired insurance policy. A stroke of genius, that. With one small accident he had placed the cab driver exactly where Lizina wanted him. He had helped another client rid himself of a Comet Q90-T that was a certified lead-plated dog. At a profit!

The Q90-T was an unbelievably beautiful car. It also had the notorious reputation of being a clunker.

Yemahl had no doubt his firm would win the suit against Mikk.

As for Thax Wilanu—Yemahl had done quite well there also. While he had not drained the man of his last stell—yet—Thax's credaccount was down to a thousand stells. For a man accustomed to living on the edge of his means, a single stell and a thousand had about the same buying power.

Yemahl buttoned off the monitor. It had been a good two weeks. Lizina would be pleased with all he had achieved in such a short time. Nothing short of a miracle, he told himself with no strain in patting his broad and padded back.

She would be especially interested in learning that Thax had contacted *Forerunner* today. The man was obviously seeking financial aid from his sometime business partner . . . Captain Kukis.

14

Lizina had stared into the face of the Bogey Man, and she had survived. For two weeks! (It seemed two years.)

Bogar opened the envelope she handed him. A thick, black eyebrow arched high. His eyes narrowed suspiciously when he raised them at his pupil.

"What's this? I've already checked my credaccount. You've paid me in full . . . Captain!"

That last, single word came as a softened growl (still a growl, but less throaty). It was the closest thing to a compliment Bogar had ever uttered during his time onboard *Windrammer*. Lizina beamed.

"Call it a bonus for a job well done."

Then she was staring. She didn't believe it, but Bogar appeared to be embarrassed.

Impishly, she added to his obvious discomfort by leaning forward and kissing his cheek. The result was a delight. After two weeks of verbal harassment from the Bogey Man, it was a pleasure to watch him squirm a bit.

"Thanks." Bogar gruffed. He held up the envelope and nodded. "Now I've a shuttle to catch and a ship of my own to attend."

Bogar walked to the door of the con-cabin. He paused with stubby legs astraddle the hatchway and glanced back to Lizina.

"You've still got a lot of learnin' to get inside that stubborn head of yours. And if you don't go off and get yourself killed, you'll learn it. Lizina, you're worthy of the spaceways and so's your ship. Take care of both!''

Before Lizina recovered from the unexpected praise, Bogar was gone. Tears welled in her eyes.

Sentimental and unwarranted! She chided herself on her overreaction to Bogar's words.

She didn't care. She would miss the crusty old bastard. The spaceways had its share of Kukises and Ganesas. But as long as there were Bogars plying the Tachyon Trail, the race that called itself Galactic would be worthy of the stars it conquered.

If the gods humankind worshipped truly existed, she hoped they smiled their fortune on a spacefarer who bore the uncomplimentary nickname Bogey Man.

Lizina left the offices of Huhleem, Sudi, Tabir, Yutu, Kwam & Progeny less than certain of herself. Until now it had been a game. Thax and Mikk were always in the future.

But tonight . . . tonight they would be very real.

She caught herself. *Has my short return to freedom softened me? Have I forgotten what these two pigs did to me?*

They had sold her like a piece of meat. To them she had not been a human being. Her life, her dreams, her desires had been meaningless to them. They had seen her as merchandise, goods for their profit. A high-class stash to be sold into slavery. And they had seen to it—to their mutual profit.

What had happened to her—the abuse, the degradation, the humiliation she had been forced to endure (and survive!)—had meant nothing to those two.

For her to consider Thax Wilanu and his cohort Mikk human was stupidity on her part. To allow either of the swine to walk the streets would be a crime equal to their own.

Lizina had no intention of committing that crime.

*   *   *

Chane watched Lizina step from the shower. He tried to think of Hoku and the dreams they shared. The spritely bounce of his employer's bosom, the shapely curves of her naked buttocks, her long, beckoning calves and thighs, and the baby-bare, hairless mound of her stash—like that of most Galactics, Lizina's body bore no hair other than that atop her head—made it mighty hard. Harder than he liked to admit.

Lizina moved to her dressing table and began brushing the shoulder-length cascade of her copper-hued hair. Her reflection in the mirror smiled at her First Mate.

"Did you meet with Captain Catava?"

"Pos." Chane nodded. "All the arrangements have been made. She'll be ready to receive the . . . uh . . . cargo onboard *OlSwifty* any time after midnight."

"Good." Lizina opened a round box atop the dressing table. From it she lifted a raven-black wig. She held it up for Chane. "Like it?"

He shrugged.

"Such enthusiasm!"

"Lizina . . . are you certain you want to go through with this?"

"I've never been more certain of anything in my life. Thax and Mikk deserve what I will give them tonight, Chane. If you doubt it, just think of Mahir and how he used me."

Lizina dropped the wig back into the box. She pushed her own hair atop her head, twisted it, pinned it in place. Again she brought out the wig. This time she put it on. Staring at her reflection in the mirror, she settled it carefully in place.

She smiled. Thax would never recognize her under this mop of black ringlets. The idea for her disguise as would-be heiress Cilehe Luister was something she had picked up from Dorjan.

If he remembers me at all!

Her gaze shifted from her own altered reflection to Chane. Worry still lined his brow. Those nascent furrows made her aware of his youth, and her own experience. It made her feel old, old.

"Chane, you don't owe me anything. If you want out, you know you can leave any time you wish. There *are* certain elements of danger in what we're planning. If the policers should somehow get wind of what we're up to . . ."

"No! It's not that. I'm not afraid of the policers!"

"You should be. What we're going to do tonight is as illegal as anything they've done." She paused in her chiding.

Chane's expression hadn't changed. Staring at her, he seemed on the point of being sick.

He's not worried about tonight. Grabbles, what is eating at him?

She had no more asked herself the question when the answer wormed into her head. That wasn't worry on his face—it was embarrassment!

About what?

An amused smile tugged at the corners of her mouth as her gaze shifted to her own reflection. Without comment, she rose and walked to her closet. She selected a robe both opaque and long. She wrapped it about her nakedness. Chastely covered, she looked at him. And at that instant she *knew*.

"It's Hoku, isn't it?"

Chane's head jerked around. His eyes were wide with surprise.

Lizina smiled. Did men think women were blind? Or just stupid?

"How . . . long have you known?"

"Since she came onboard *Windrammer*. You couldn't keep your eyes off her. Or your hands, right?"

"Lizina . . . I . . . why didn't you say something?" The little boy in him dominated his voice and expression.

"There was no need to, Chane. I don't own you—or you me. You've been sharing my bed because *I* offered and *you* accepted. I never said it was anything more than that." Taken alone, her words were cold. Lizina's tone accompanied them, gentled them.

She walked to Chane and lightly touched his cheek. "I've always been honest with you. Told you of the man I'm searching for. The child I carry. His child."

"Your mystery man?"

"He's not that mysterious." Lizina smiled. "And if you feel for Hoku half of what I feel for him, you'd be a fool to let her get away."

Chane grinned and shook his head in disbelief.

"There's an empty cabin on *Windrammer*. If it will make things more convenient, it's yours. Ship's First Mate needs his own room." Lizina returned the grin.

Chane's arms encircled her in a bearish hug. "Lizina, I *do* love you!"

"Don't let Hoku hear that!" Lizina disentangled herself from his arms. "Now redshift and let me dress. I've got an important date tonight."

Chane started to the door of her room.

She called after him. "You and Boldua have the cook prepare you dinner. I'll be dining at the *Lal Autar* tonight!"

"Right, Captain!" Chane winked as he left.

Lizina shook her head. *First time I ever lost a man to another woman—and felt good about it!*

The cab halted before the *Lal Autar*. While Lizina dug into a beaded evening bag for her credcard, she saw a metallic gray floater pull to the curb on the opposite side of the street. Chane and Boldua were both visible inside the aqua-tinted bubble. Her bodyguards for the night—and her partners in crime.

While the cabbie inserted the card into the credslot of the taxi's console, she glanced at the two and nodded to acknowledge their presence. She dropped the returned credcard back into her evening bag and stepped from the cab.

She was dressed to kill in a Tulann's design purchased solely for this night. The gown was very black and backless down to here. The halter front offered a neckline that more than plunged; it dived. Down the satiny valley of the shadow of her breasts it plunged to reveal the fascinating well of navel. The slash stopped just above Panish's legal definition of indecent exposure.

The skirt (floor length) was a series of over-lapping diamond-shaped panels connected at the waist. The panels shifted with her every movement to reveal provocative glimpses of remarkably shapely legs caressed in black net hose. Spiked heels (black) enhanced the turn of calves she very well knew were alluring to begin with.

Lizina entered the club, past the two human doormen and allowed the maitre d' to escort her into the *Lal Autar*'s red-lit, circular bar. Her glance roved the room as if casually.

Her pulse doubled.

Thax was there. Seated alone on the far side of the room. He stared at her.

Lizina's gaze passed him by as though unnoticed. She was not supposed to know him. Not yet. Thax was to take the initiative and contact Cilehe Luister. The first move was up to him.

And if it didn't go as planned . . . then Chane and Boldua waited outside to provide another form of persuasion to convince the slimy sisterslicer of the need to cooperate.

Lizina crossed the room to a vacant table near Thax. She felt naked, although the sensation did not originate in the undisguised stares that followed her movements.

For the first time since escaping Mirjam, Lizina was without a stopper.

Thax moved quickly. He was at her table before a waitress took her order.

"Cilehe? Cilehe Luister? Is that you?" He took a chair without invitation. "It's me—Thax Wilanu. Don't you recognize me?"

Damn right I do, you sisterslicing swine!

"Thax! It can't be! It's been at least five years!" She played the prearranged charade to the hilt.

Her heart (imitating a bass drum) lodged itself in her throat. What if he *did* recognize her? The Shadow Walker-style disguise had seemed a perfect touch that afternoon. Now it seemed thin; even transparent.

Thax waved for drinks and waited until the waitress brought them before leaning toward Lizina with a wide grin. "I believe we have a mutual acquaintance."

Damn, but he's an attractive devil!

She had forgotten just how attractive. It was easy to understand how she had accepted this man without question that long-ago night in this very club. Then she had searched for a casual lover for the night. She still wanted him this night—but for totally different reasons.

She nodded. "It is my understanding that you have a talent for . . . shall we say . . . helping people disappear."

He took a non-committal sip of his drink.

"It is also my understanding that certain unforeseen circumstances have placed you in a financially binding situation."

He winced at that, but managed to say nothing. He was working to radiate charm and confidence, and Lizina damned well knew it.

"There is a person whose disappearance—sudden disappearance—would be financially beneficial to both you and me."

"Our mutual acquaintance explained the situation,"

he said to the table. "Siblings can be troublesome. Especially when they stand in the way of a sizable inheritance." Thax smiled coolly as he took another sip from his glass. Yes, glass; there was no plass in *Lal Autar*.

There was also no "mutual acquaintance." One of Thax's "friends" had arranged the meeting (thanks to one of Yemahl Huhleem's investigators and a hefty increase in that friend's credaccount).

"Then . . . you can aid me?"

Lizina sensed his hunger. Not for her, but for cash. Thax was hurting. Yemahl had seen to that.

"I've already made certain contacts to expedite matters." He glanced around. "But this is not the place to discuss business. My place . . ."

Lizina shook her head. "My place."

Thax smiled (oh-such a seductive smile) and nodded.

"It is also my understanding that you work with a partner." (Lizina saw his eyes narrow slightly, but he covered fast.) "I would also like to meet him."

"I'm afraid that is impossible. My partner prefers to remain in the wings." Thax shrugged. "I'm certain you can understand. He is in a delicate position."

"And I'm certain you can understand my reluctance to finalize such a large transaction without meeting the parties involved." Lizina's voice was firm. "It has been an enjoyable evening. But I'm afraid I must be going."

She didn't give him a chance to reply. She rose and walked from the bar without looking back. Very aware of eyes on her, she was sure that one pair was not watching her only because of her sexy attire. Thax's eyes.

Thax caught up with her outside.

"If you'll give me time enough for a call, I'll see if my friend can meet us . . . at *your* place." There was an ugly gray tinge of desperation in Thax's voice. He had almost let her get away and he knew it.

Lizina gave him her address and agreed to wait while he made the call. When he re-entered the *Lal Autar* to phone his friend, Lizina glanced to the men still waiting across the street. Chane and Boldua. She winked.

Everything was going as scheduled.

Chane entered the room in a tight-fitting butler's uniform of burgundy. He carried in a silver tray decorated with three champagne glasses. He nodded approval as Lizina took the one on the right. The remaining two he served to Thax and Mikk.

She waited until Chane left before standing and raising her glass to the two visitors to the Harith estate. "To my sister. May she live her life on a planet that's never heard of Panish!"

Her meeting with the two had been brief. They had agreed on a price for the bogus kidnapping. Then Thax had sent a message to Captain Kukis, presently docked at Lanatia . . . a touch suggested by Yemahl Huhleem. Kukis—with, presumably, First Mate Degula—would be at Panishport in five days to pick up the . . . special cargo.

Thax and Mikk stood and lifted their drinks. They waited until Lizina drank, then emptied their glasses.

"Undoubtedly Qalaran." Thax pursed his lips. "The flavor is unmistakable. But there's a subtle undercurrent of sweetness that eludes me. Was it from a new vineyard?"

"It wasn't a standard Qalaran vintage. The vine was fortified." Lizina smiled innocently. "With Sleeper."

"Sleeper! I don't believe . . ." Shock froze Thax's features. "Sleeper!"

"A knockout belt?" Mikk's own disbelief outdid his partner's.

"You bitch! I don't know what you think you're up

to, but you won't get away with it!'' Thax started
toward her, hands outstretched to wring her lovely neck.

"That's far enough!'' Chane's voice came from behind the enraged man.

Thax whirled. So did Mikk. Chane and Boldua stood
there, stoppers leveled at the two men. Chane was even
smiling.

"Their guns are set on One.'' Lizina's voice drew
her guests' attention back to her. "I've no intention of
killing you. That would be too easy.''

"What's going on here?'' This from Mikk. "Why a
Sleeper? I ain't never done ya no wrong, lady. Why?''

Lizina reached up and wrenched the black wig from
her head. Next the pins came out. She shook her head.
The long, silky strands of her own hair tumbled lightly
about her shoulders and flashed in the light.

"Wait a min! I've seen ya! You're the stash we sold
to . . .''

"Shut up, Mikk!'' Thax glared at his cohort in the
flesh trade. Then he looked back at Lizina.

Thax recognized her, too. She could see it in those
dark, frightened eyes. She smiled. That he knew her,
realized what he had done to her, made the moment all
the more satisfying.

"What . . . do you intend to do?'' Thax's voice had
lost all traces of composure. Sweat beaded his forehead.
Thax Wilanu looked as if he had swallowed something
distinctly unpleasant.

He had.

"That would spoil the surprise.'' Her smile grew
wickedly. "I promise you that *I* won't kill you. Nor
will I sell you to Kukis. I wouldn't do that to a vug!''

Lizina looked at Chane. "Get them into jumpsuits
before the Sleeper takes effect. I'll go upstairs and
change.''

With one last appraising gaze at her two captives,

Lizina turned and walked rustling toward the house's elevators.

So far so good. They both fell for it without a question!

She made a mental note to see that Yemahl and his investigators received a nice bonus for their efficiency.

To Harmony's shuttleport officials, drunken (or stoned) spacefarers were common. That *Windrammer*'s shapely captain had to help carry two of her crew, both unconscious, onboard was far from unusual. Better they were all offplanet.

Passed-out spacefarers were even less a rarity within Panishport. Lizina and her crewmates—along with the two unconscious companions they lugged between them—received even less notice. Nor did anyone question the fact that the five moved down a tunnel that took them in the opposite direction from their ship's berth.

Captain Catava of Corsi did notice their approach to her ship. The tall, rangy woman and two of her all-female crew greeted them at the open hatch to *OlSwifty*. Catava ordered her crewmembers to help Chane and Boldua take the two "passengers" to their quarters (a converted hold; Catava often carried "passengers").

Lizina handed her fellow spacefarer a fat envelope. Catava hefted it twice, but left it unopened.

"I feel a bit guilty about taking this. After all, my two *passengers* will more than pay for themselves."

Lizina noted that the Corser made no attempt to return the stells.

"They'll bring a good price on Bleak. Twice what I could get for them elsewhere. I owe you, Lizina." Catava winked at her fellow captain. "Care to come onboard for a drink?"

"Maybe next time you're in Panishport. Tonight lasted at least a year."

Catava sucked at her teeth. "Too bad. My girls and I enjoy entertaining guests."

I'll just bet you do!

Catava's lingering gaze left no doubt in Lizina's mind as to what type of entertainment the captain of *OlSwifty* had planned.

Chane and Boldua stepped from the hatch. Chane nodded.

"The passengers have been tucked away for the night, Captain."

"Maybe next time, Catava." Lizina smiled at the tall woman.

"Maybe next time." Catava flipped her fingers in that universal gesture of spacefarers: "maybe."

With Chane and Boldua to either side of her, Lizina walked back toward *Windrammer*'s berth. It *had* been a long night. And a good one!

Oh yes a good one, she thought, full of tingles of excitement.

Bleak?

She had never heard of the planet. She would have to read up on it. With luck it would live up to its ominous name. She would hate to think Thax and Mikk had been sold as slaves on some paradise planet.

Bleak.

She smiled. All but two names were now scratched off her mental list. The Chank Captain Kukis and his Mate Degula were all who remained. For those two, bondage wouldn't be enough. Lizina had something special prepared to repay the agony they had given her—an eternity of pain!

15

Pascal was a barren star. Planetless, its sole notable feature was an asteroid belt orbiting at a mean radius of 4.65^8 kloms from the star's surface. The belt was rich in deposits of aluminum. Once, Galactics mined the jagged chunks of rock afloat about Pascal.

That was before the development of unipolymer plasteel and other quasi-metals with their advantages of being both lighter and stronger than the natural element (as well as entailing far less in production costs).

Humankind left but one reminder of ever having touched the little-known star system. An abandoned space colony carved within the interior of a five-klom-long asteroid. The colony's original name (if it had ever borne one) had been forgotten with the passage of the decades. Or perhaps it had been centuries.

For the past eight years, since its discovery by the escaped Harbian slaves Dorjan and Songan, it had carried the name HOME (Habitat Orbiter: Modular Environment), which had been taken from a brass (not prass) identification tag found on the back of one of the colony's computing units.

HOME no longer sheltered miners from the infinitely yawning chasm of space. Now it harbored one hundred and sixty escaped slaves—fifty fewer than before Ganesa of Resh's treacherous attack on the colony. Each of these men and women had been freed of bondage by *Misfit*'s crew and offered a new life HOME.

Few refused the opportunity.

Those who did were brainwiped of any knowledge of *Misfit*, crew, and HOME, and set free on a planet of their choosing. Thus were HOME's secret and security maintained.

In eight years only one person had stumbled upon the asteroid colony—Ganesa of Resh. She and her crew were no longer around to tell of the discovery, because they were no longer on the spaceways. Dorjan had sent Ganesa's ship *Be Lively* (captain and crew onboard) Forty Per Cent City. They had not been heard from since.

It was here, to HOME, that *Misfit* and crew returned after their escape from Ginneh. Home to the refuge hidden amid the cosmic debris circling the nearly unknown star Pascal.

Dorjan stood on the balcony of his quarters in HOME. His gaze lovingly ran over the countryside that stretched before him like a dream of spring come true.

For a newcomer the view often brought swirling vertigo and spatial disorientation.

HOME was a cylinder that lay on its curved side. A plethora of buildings, trees, plants, and small lakes covered the walls and seemed to defy gravity by hanging suspended, upside down. From the ceiling!

They didn't. HOME rotated to create centrifugal force and the illusion of gravity (point-six normal).

"Listen to this!"

Dorjan turned. Songan sat at a monitor scanning a backlog of news reports that had been missed during their time on Mirjam and Ginneh. The items often provided the basic groundwork for The Invisible One's next job.

Dorjan steeled himself for some new scheme involving the galaxy's master thief. Assuming the role of The Shadow Walker was the farthest thing from his mind, despite the fact that cash was needed to repair the damages to HOME wrought by Ganesa's attack.

Dorjan's mind had been on Panish—and Lizina. Booda, but he ached for her!

"It's only a minor item. But I thought you might find it interesting." Songan looked back to the monitor and read:

"**GINNEH**—Transgalactic Watch Destrier *Fearless* under the command of Captain Gadi Luyu, raided this mining planet's sole settlement in a policing operation that uncovered a laboratory for the production of the illegal drug tetrazombase."

Songan looked up. "It goes on to say several men were arrested in the raid—names withheld until officially charged—and a cache of six kilos of TZ was confiscated."

"TGW! When?"

"Two days ago. They hit a week after our hasty departure." Songan grinned. "We could have used their help."

"Policers have a way of showing up only when they're not wanted." Dorjan shook his head. It had taken Nav only a few days after the destruction of his lab to resume production. "Wonder what put TGW on to Nav?"

"An 'anonymous communique' is all the report says." Songan flicked off the monitor. "Whoever the grat was, he or she deserves a medal!"

"I'll drink to that!" Dorjan walked in from the balcony. "I've got two Starflares tucked away. Care for one?"

Songan waved away the offer; Dorjan walked into the kitchen to retrieve a beer. He returned a moment later, plass in hand.

"Nothing for The Shadow Walker in all that?" Dorjan stretched out on a sofa and sipped at his beer.

"Huh?" Songan looked at his friend as though just noticing they were in the same room.

"The Shadow Walker? That's why you were reading the news reports, weren't you?"

Songan's chest heaved. "Pos. Didn't find anything that looked interesting."

Misfit's First Mate turned to the balcony. His dark eyes had a distant look. Once more his brainboosted genius of a mind had gone its own way, leaving Dorjan behind.

"Songan?"

The tattooed giant continued to stare into space.

"Songan?" Louder this time, bringing Songan's head back around.

"Sorry, Dorjan, my mind has been wandering lately."

"Is it Yoluta?"

Songan nodded and pursed his lips. "Part of me says she's dead. That I should accept it. Another part says there's a chance she might live again. That I've got to do everything I can to give her that chance."

Dorjan sat silently, uncertain what to say or how to comfort his friend. "Have you found anything solid to go on?"

Songan shook his head. "A few leads. Nothing definite."

"Such as?"

"To begin with, *regeneration* of the dead doesn't exist. Cloning, as we're both aware, does. Qalara is the apparent center of research. A place called Hakimit Medical Center."

Dorjan nodded. Vegetables were cloned onboard *Misfit* and HOME for food. He hadn't realized that human cloning was practical. Arena slaves were allowed to realize little. Possible, yes. But not practical, by ancient fiat. To clone the dead was directly opposed to the natural genetic evolution of humankind.

"Qalara? Captain Chicken's homeworld?"

Songan smiled and nodded. He had never heard his friend refer to Jonuta of Qalara by name—or without disgust in his voice. Though the two had never met, Dorjan's hate for the man was deep-rooted. Jonuta was a slaver. A phenomenally successful slaver.

"I want to go there, Dorjan. To the Hakimit Med Center."

"Hakimit Med Center it is. We'll stop over at Qalara on our way to Panish."

The jaunt would be out of the way, Dorjan mused, staring into his beer. But then this was Songan!

"Thank you. I know how much it means to you to get to Panish—and Lizina." Songan's voice sounded lighter now, relieved. "I should find out what I need in a couple of days onplanet."

"It'll give Varn a chance to do his shopping." Dorjan laughed. "He's holding me to my promise!"

"Might pick up tinted contacts for the rest of the crew, Dorjan. If Varn's taste runs true to form, we could all be blinded without some sort of protection!"

"Speaking of our Outie, I haven't seen him since we docked." Dorjan took another swig from his beer.

"He's been helping shift some vacant building on the eastside to this end. Replacements for those Ganesa and her crew blasted. Easier than processing a large order of aluminum on short order."

"And the other repairs?"

"Except for interior damages to buildings, HOME is relatively back to normal. The new drive is up and functional. Whenever we're ready, HOME can convert to tachyons—every atom and molecule—and subspace out of here."

"The stars!" Dorjan grinned. "The stars are going to be ours!"

It was a dream. A ship to explore the billions of stars

humankind had yet to visit. It was now a dream within the grasp of HOMErs.

One more trip in toward Galaxy Center. To Qalara—to Panish and Lizina. Then the stars!

HOME slept. Only a few lights glowed from windows throughout the cylindrical world. Through the center of the tube, stars winked at the asteroid colony (a holographic projection of the heavens beyond HOME's protective shield of metal and rock).

Edrek and Kefira walked through the artificial night. Neither touched—not even hands. Neither spoke. They merely walked.

Occasionally, Kefira's head lifted and she stared above.

Silently Edrek watched her and wondered. Did her thoughts roam to Kuzih? Surely she must feel the desire to return to her homeworld—often. Kefira *was*, after all, the only member of her race to stumble accidentally upon the Galactics' worlds.

Kuzih.

How many countless times had Edrek's own musing turned to the lost world? On each occasion Kefira spoke of her people, he had tried to imagine the planet.

It was a world populated by this totally unknown race of alien beings. The Akil. A race that possessed a rudimentary knowledge of space travel, similar to humankind's position at the beginning of the Twenty-first Century. That almost forgotten time before Galactics fared along the spaceways to the stars.

Kefira was cautiously reticent when questioned about Kuzih or its location among the billions of stars in the Galaxy's vastness. She was equally reticent to speak of her past in more than generalities.

The Akil woman had been discovered via an indecipherable radio signal SIPACUM picked up on one of *Misfit*'s sublight hops from Terasaki to Luhra eighteen months ago, more than a year before Edrek and his sister Yoluta had been rescued from slavers on Thebanis. She had been found in cryogenic suspension within a spherical lifeboat.

Dorjan and his crew revived her from cold-sleep. After an encephaloboost to provide her with the ability to speak Erts, she claimed no knowledge of how long she had been within the sphere or of how she had arrived within the Farther Reaches.

She described herself as the Akil equivalent of a human anthropologist. She had been in transit to Hjor—a planet neighboring Kuzih that the Akil had colonized—when the craft she rode developed drive problems. She had been able to make it to a lifeboat before the ship exploded, then placed herself in cryogenic suspension to await rescue by her own people. She also claimed no astronomical knowledge of Kuzih's position in the galaxy.

Edrek accepted the explanation of her advent into the worlds of humankind. He realized that his companions within HOME held unvoiced reservations about Kefira's sudden appearance—and her purpose for being among Galactics—despite the fact that the Akil had never given any indication that she was more or less than she claimed.

Does she yearn for Kuzih now? Edrek wondered, while he studied the beauty of Kefira's uplifted face.

Or does she remember Ginneh?

He prayed to Booda that it was the former. In his heart, he knew it was the latter.

Since Kefira's rescue from Mensah Nav and *Misfit*'s escape from the hostile jungle world, Kefira had been strangely distant. In that time they had made love only once.

Made love?

Only in the broadest of connotations!

The union had lacked the joy and mutual caring of reunited lovers, of any semblance of love. It had been a singularly mechanical act. Even physically Kefira had seemed to be light-years away.

Makhseem. The Akil word niggled into his head. It roughly translated into Erts as fornicate. It meant more—oh so much more! Kefira had taught him that. It was the sharing of body and soul between a man and a woman. *Makhseem.* The total giving of oneself—mentally, emotionally, and physically.

Edrek had not asked what had occurred during the months since Ganesa had kidnapped Kefira from HOME and sold her as a slave to Mensah Nav. When the time was right, when everything was sorted in her mind, Kefira would tell him.

When the time is right—if it ever will be again!

He tried to push the uncertainty aside. He couldn't. Doubts riddled his every thought. The love they had shared before Ganesa, before Ginneh and Nav, now seemed to have belonged to two totally different people. Two imagined people.

Edrek reached out and lightly stroked the white-gold of her flowing hair. "Kefira . . ."

"What?" Startled, she jerked around. Her lemur-round eyes were twice as wide as usual.

"I didn't mean to frighten you. I just want to talk."

Kefira took his hand in both of hers. She squeezed it tightly, then lifted it to her lips. Her gaze met his, then her eyes seemed to burn.

"There is much we must talk of, my love. I thought that I could find the answers alone. Once, perhaps, I would have been able to do so. That was before you. You, my love, have jumbled the rational thoughts of a very orderly mind."

That elated Edrek, but he said only, "Is it about Ginneh?" The words came with hesitance.

A perplexed frown twisted Kefira's face. "Ginneh?"

The confused expression evaporated and was replaced by an amused smile. She realized what Edrek meant, now. How could she explain to him? To the Akil the concepts of physical and sexual dominance and abuse were unknown, as alien as she was to these people who audaciously called themselves Galactics.

The acts Nav had required her to perform for him— for his men (while he watched)—were not degrading. Not to an Akil. They too were *makhseem*. She had given her body to her captor willingly. Had found pleasure with him.

She was not what Galactics called a hust (a concept as ungraspable to Kefira as the true meaning of *makhseem* was to this often confusing, furless race). An Akil, male or female, gave whatever was needed to whomever was in need. There was no corresponding word to "hust" in the Akil tongue, or "harlot." There were no husts, either. Sex was not a commodity for the selling, or rather the renting out, one piece at a time.

Edrek's hand still cradled in hers, she said, "I'll try to explain all that has been a jumble in my mind while we return to our rooms."

Edrek nodded. Finally she was willing to talk!

"My love, please lay Ginneh behind you. Rest assured that in Galactic terms, I was not abused while I was with Mensah Nav. The only pain he or Ganesa caused was the ache of being separated from you. Neither of them physically—or mentally—harmed me."

She glanced at the young man from Lanatia. Relief washed over his face. He smiled at her.

"If Ginneh hasn't been bothering you—then what?" Edrek's hand slipped from her furred one. His arm went about her narrow waist. She offered no protest.

"Kuzih," Kefira answered simply. "Please listen while I try to explain. I'm afraid . . . I fear that I am not what I have appeared to be, my love. It may take some time to . . . place matters in their correct perspective."

Edrek started to reply, but held back the hundred questions that rushed into his mind. He did as she requested. Edrek hushed, and he listened.

He listened all the way back to their rooms and for an hour after that. His mind staggered with each new revelation Kefira uttered. He had readily accepted the story of her seemingly miraculous pure-chance appearance among his people.

But this!

He shook his head in disbelief when she concluded.

"I don't know what to say. I need time to think it over. To sort through everything."

She nodded and her eyes were full of empathy. "Now you can understand my confusion."

He could!

"I have tried to convince myself that I was alone in this. That the decision was mine and only mine. But it isn't. You, my love, must also share in that decision."

Edrek nodded. And what a decision! She offered him more than just herself. It was a new way of life!

Kefira smiled. "I feel as though I have been walking with two gees tugging at me for the past week. Now, sharing this with you has me in null-gee. I was wrong to shut you out of my life. I have grown to need you. I even tried to deny *makhseem* between us."

She rose from beside him on the sofa. "And that was terribly wrong. For you. And for me."

Kefira's softly furred hands touched the neck of the yellow HOMEspun (a fiberglas manufactured in the colony) jumpsuit. The molecular binding opened.

"Kefira altRusalka would delight in *makhseem* with you, my love."

She edged the jumpsuit from her shoulders and wiggled it down over very femininely curved hips. Stepping from the clothing, she kicked it away and stood before him unashamed of her nakedness. Or her need for this man.

Edrek's gaze caressed the unveiled beauty of the . . . alien body. *My woman's body*, he mentally corrected. *Alien is a word*.

She was exotic—and more than erotic.

Fine pale gold-white down (a shade deeper than her silky hair) sleeked her supple body. Her breasts—like ripened sweetfruits—stood high on her chest; higher than a Galactic woman's. Each was tipped by a small delicate-looking nipple, coral pink in hue. The tiny buds and the surrounding aureoles were devoid of soft fur. The mound of her sex, too, appeared almost Galactic in its lack of hair, and was perhaps two shades pinker than her nipples.

Edrek stood. His hands rose to remove his own clothing. Kefira brushed them away, preferring to undertake the task herself with "perfectly normal" hands of four fingers plus opposed thumb.

He did not mind. His hands found other matters to attend. Kefira's chest thrust forward in a less than subtle manner to assure him the attention was appreciated.

Her golden saucer eyes shifted upward to capture his gaze. An almost innocent smile tugged the corners of her mouth. Pale lavender, her tongue flicked behind her parted lips.

Edrek's stroking palms tightened to draw her to him for a passionate kiss. He stopped himself before carrying through with that natural *human* desire.

Kefira was not human.

The mouth-to-mouth kiss was not shared by the Akil.

Other, more intimate kisses were. Kefira apparently intended to demonstrate that fact, once again. She began to sink to her knees before her now-naked human lover.

Edrek's hand released the firmness of her downy warheads and grasped her shoulders. His head moved from side to side, then tilted to the recently vacated sofa.

Her smile widening, Kefira stretched atop the sofa and opened her arms to him. Edrek came to her, into her. Her soft moan echoed his own when he entered the liquid warmth of her body.

His weight marvelously pressed atop her, she held him tightly, savoring that first moment of their union, the fullness of his presence within her body.

She had shared *makhseem* with others, both Akil and Galactic. She had known the enthusiastic lovemaking of Songbird the Jarp who was both man and woman. Each race in its own way had been exciting and had brought pleasures to her body and sensuous mind.

But with Edrek there were differences exceeding the obvious differences in human and Akil. And that too was *makhseem*—the sharing of body and soul with one who was loved.

When HOME's artificial dawn awoke the asteroid colony, Edrek and Kefira still lay atop the sofa locked within one another's arms. They had also made a mutual decision about Kuzih.

Dorjan stared at Kefira. His eyes shifted toward a grinning Edrek, then back to the Akil woman. Kefira's lemur-round eyes did not flinch from his.

He shook his head and took a deep breath. The two had given him a hell of a lot to assimilate in the past thirty minutes!

"Are you angered by my deception?"

Dorjan looked back at Kefira and grinned. Anger was the last thing he felt. "No! Shocked. Dazed. But not angry."

And who wouldn't be dazed after hearing what he had just heard? Kuzih wasn't a single planet. It was a confederation of five worlds!

And *three* alien races!

The bird-descended Leitii—wingless, and without a trace of plumage. The Sisika, whom Kefira described as winged, metamorphic, and having three sexes. And the Akil!

The Kuzih had more than rudimentary spaceflight. They had developed a drive similar to the double P. Two Galactic-standard years ago, a Kuzih spacer had come upon a disabled Galactic vessel; *Lightrider*. The ship had been attacked by pirates. All but three of the crew had been killed. The human survivors were taken into "protective custody." They were now being held on Kefira's homeworld Pilisi.

Dorjan admitted "custody" and "held" might be overly harsh terms. The three had been given unrestricted access to the Kuzih planets and had apparently displayed no urgent desire to return to the Galactic worlds.

From information obtained from *Lightrider*'s survivors, Kefira and three other Akil had been set adrift inward of Barbro in the hope that their lifeboats would be discovered by passing spacers.

News reports had given no indication that the other three had been discovered.

Simply put, Kefira of Akil was a spy.

Her task was to gather what information she could about Galactic civilization. The Kuzih had no wish to make their presence known to a race that had claimed nearly two hundred worlds; such a race might also wish to claim their planets.

And now Kefira offered to lead Dorjan to the Kuzih worlds.

"Well," Edrek said, and stared at his captain and respected friend in youthful anticipation. "What do you intend to do?"

Dorjan laughed again. The Lanatian sounded as if he expected an immediate response—action. Dorjan's brain was still attempting a macro-sorting of all the marvelous alien images Kefira's revelations had implanted.

"The first thing I intend to do is get Songan over here. Then I plan to sit there and watch his face while you two repeat everything you've just told me. After that . . . we'll see.''

Still laughing, he rose and moved to the phone to call his First Mate.

Dorjan really had no doubt about the "after that." HOME was ready for the voyage. And the Kuzih worlds were waiting, tucked silently away among the billions of stars humankind had yet to explore! (Billions, yes. How many Akil? How many races peopled the spaceway?)

It would take time to prepare HOMErs for the voyage. Time—and stells—to insure that the colony/ship had everything needed for the journey. But there was no doubt in Dorjan's mind that HOME now had a destination for her maiden voyage!

16

Ganesa of Resh sat in the captain's chair of *Be Lively*. She glared at the control console. To stare was all she could do. Ninety per cent of the unit was dead.

The other ten percent of her spacer's systemry was dying.

Be Lively's single functioning optic was trained on the killer that slowly drained the ship's life. The monstrously large orb crowded every screen. A planet.

What the Diamond Lady saw in the two-dimensional image was exactly all she knew about the world her ship orbited. SIPACUM was down.

Down, hell! It's dead! Gone forever!

Her computrician had pronounced the unit's fate two days ago.

He had opened SIPACUM's compact frame and stared within for two minutes before uttering a sound. And even then it was only a horrified groan.

Every tetra-bubble in the unit was melted!

Minute pools of melted and recrystallized memory chips (a misnomer for the bubble crystals that had remained in computerese from a long-forgotten era) splotched each panel he pulled from SIPACUM. The majority could be replaced from ship's stores, he assured her. For those that couldn't he could jury-rig replacements.

The 8901100-LLP40 bus was completely ruined, also. Yet it, too, he could replace. Though he offered no explanation or even speculation as to the nature of the force that had so mangled *Be Lively*'s brain, he showed confidence.

The computrician had performed all that he said he would. It took him twenty-four around-the-chron hours.

Then he had buttoned on the power, ready to burn the code into SIPACUM's ROM (Read Only Memory) chips. Burn he did. The problem was, the horror was, that he would never be sure of just what memory codes he had burned into SIPACUM, or where.

Overlooked in his inspection was one small component; the Qalaran-made JWWN3298 interpretator. Small . . . and entirely essential. The interpretator accepted encoded NORMAL (Nuance Oriented Rational Memory-Analog Language: the standardized computer language along the spaceways) and translated it into SIPACUM's tetradecimal machine language. Only one in a thousand computricians who traveled the parsec abyss could speak to SIPACUM in its own tongue.

Ganesa's computrician was not that one in a thousand.

SIPACUM was dead, unable to perform even the simplest of calculations.

The computrician was now locked in his cabin attempting to assemble a simple binary computer from SIPACUM's useless parts. Whether Ganesa would ever get to view the results was unlikely.

The mistress of *Be Lively* glanced back to the planet held focused by her ship's single eye. She could only guess at its name—if it had one—or its location. Nor did she know whether its atmosphere was suitable for human life. Or the gravity of this world. Or if it was inhabited.

All she knew for certain was what she could see in the two-dimensional image. The planet was big. It had oceans . . . at least eighty per cent of the surface was water, if she estimated correctly. And there were two continents. Possibly four, if the polar icecaps were included. She didn't include them.

There was one other fact she knew about this big world, although the information was not held in the visual image. Like every other body in the galaxy, the world had a gravitational pull.

Gravity: considered the weakest force in the universe. Now that "weak" force that was killing *Be Lively*.

And will kill me!

Ganesa didn't consider the six remaining members of her crew who would die in the process. There were other crews, waiting to be hired. There was only one Ganesa of Resh.

For two days *Be Lively* had circled the unknown planet in an ever-decreasing orbit of decay. Within the hour, the ship would be drawn irrevocably into the world's atmosphere.

And there was nothing Ganesa or her crew could do about it.

"Sisterslicing scum!"

She cursed aloud although no one was within the con-cabin with her. Ganesa was very alone.

The object of her hate was a certain Captain Dasan. The two men who had done this to her had been in Dasan's employment. *They* had wrought this evil on her precious ship.

All because of one sweetcake!

"Jarp-loving bitch!" She now cursed the woman she knew as Coppertop. The one she had reclaimed from the asteroid colony in the Pascal System. "May Gri devour your soul and that of your lover!"

She called upon the dark, bloody deity of her homeworld Resh. A god she feared she would stand before in judgment all too soon. Ganesa slammed a fist down on the arm of her con-chair.

Dasan and Coppertop. Coppertop and Dasan. How

many times in the past two days had their names looped through her brain?

It was Dasan's hired killers who had slipped onboard *Be Lively*, left her and her crew bound and gagged, then jam-crammed the ship into subspace. The process was called Forty Per Cent City. Forty percent was the odds of non-survival. She had beaten those odds. Gri knew that she had felt the breath of Death on her neck, but she had beaten those odds!

When *Be Lively* jam-crammed, there had been that instant of physical and mental disequilibrium that always accompanied a jump. Only this moment had lasted an eternity!

The universe had gone gray. Ganesa could find no other words to describe the monotonous gray that had engulfed her. A vastness and a nothingness. *Be Lively* had no longer existed. She had no longer existed. The gray *was*. And was, and was. And that was all.

Then *Be Lively* was in "real" space. It had escaped Forty Per Cent City . . . to orbit this giant planet in an ever-inward spiral. Somewhere.

How long *Be Lively* had remained in the gray—the limbo of nothingness that had enshrouded it—Ganesa did not know. Every chronometer on the ship was dead.

SIPACUM was dead. Two of her crew were dead.

So was the drive. Dead! Both faster-than-light and sublight drives were become shining scrap.

Dead—but not irreparably so.

All ten polarization cells had been damaged. (Four were destroyed). Fifty per cent of the circuitry in the tachyon conversion unit so essential to the transformation of matter into those relativity-defying particles had been burned out. Fried, too, were the solar gathers, the power cells required to provide the massive energy required for tachyon conversion.

All, however, could be replaced. All that was needed

was the know-how, and the time. Just those two factors, and one was in short supply.

Aside from her computrician (and Ganesa, of course) her crew had been working within the engine's shielding for the past two days. They were completing the work far ahead of what was considered normal repair time for such extensive damage.

And it isn't fast enough! she thought, staring at that hated ball, a planetary mass so big it would gulp the falling *Be Lively* without a belch.

At least two weeks, non-stop, were needed to bring the drive on-line.

Two weeks! Gri, be merciful!

Be Lively had only minutes remaining to it. That was the measure of Ganesa's lifetime.

With an operational drive; with a makeshift computer many would consider one step beyond an abacus; with Gri's unholy blessing, the Diamond Lady might—just might—have been able to save her ship.

But with only maneuvering rockets, Ganesa saw little hope. Without a computer she would be unable to read *Be Lively*'s trajectory when it entered the atmosphere of the planet looming before it.

Ganesa pushed from her chair. She glanced down at the simple zebra-striped body stocking she wore. She grimaced. Her attire was not appropriate. If she were to stand before the dark god of Resh, it would be in her finest. With *diamonds* real on each finger. Maybe two.

After all, appearance is everything.

Even to a cruel god—she prayed.

As she turned toward the con-cabin's door, it hissed open. Her computrician entered. A wide grin ran from one side of his face to the other.

"I did it! It's not much, Captain. And the interpretator is limited. But it works! It'll compute!"

Ganesa stared at him as though uncertain what he

meant. She did. Shock dazed her. *A computer!* With it there was a possibility. A slim one!—but a possibility.

"Will it interface with the scans and the sensors?"

"It should. Though no more than three at a time. It is limited."

"Limited or not, get it on-line! Now!" Ganesa moved to the con and opened intraship comm. "All hands, close the drive-housing immediately. Then find yourself a sturdy place to cling onto for your life. Thirty minutes to planetfall. And it's going to be one hell of a rough ride!"

Toeing off the comm, she hastened from the con-cabin toward her own cabin—her room, her *chamber*. Thirty minutes wasn't long, but it was enough. When she took *Be Lively* down, it would be in her finest gown and jewels!

17

One minute after the docking collars closed about *Forerunner* to lock the ship into its Panishport berth, Lizina knew of the spacer's arrival. Such a feat was accomplished simply. She merely greased the bureaucratic gears with an ample application of stells.

Her immediate impulse was to take stopper in hand and rush to the berth, wait impatiently until the hatch opened, and fry Captain Kukis and Degula as they stepped forth.

It was only an impulse.

Instead she sent Chane to the berth with orders to report on the pair's movements every half-hour. With the last two names on her list so close, she had no intention of losing them accidentally.

While her First Mate went about his spying task, Captain Lizina retired to her room and summoned Hoku. Before Lizina could open her closet and pull out her attire for the evening, the young Terasak entered the cabin.

"Wheeew!" Lizina whistled as she glimpsed her computrician. "That is one eye-catching outfit!"

Hoku's eyes lowered demurely. But she smiled, obviously pleased by her captain's compliment.

"When we're through tonight, I'd pack that away carefully. Hold it in reserve. Then, should Chane's eye rove, pull it out. One look at you in that and he'll forget all other women!"

Hoku's smile grew.

Lizina twirled a finger for the young woman to turn around. Hoku did, and brought another whistle of approval from *Windrammer*'s captain.

While not the appropriate attire for such high-society night spots as the *Lal Autar*, the concoction would definitely do the trick tonight. Hoku wore a body-stocking that was a shade tighter than skin, in lavender Webweave. And she wore ultra-spiked crysplas heels.

Hoku wore nothing else.

The wide weave of the fabric made that fact more than evident. The network subtly gathered in enticing patches that completely veiled all vital areas of her body. It was an effect that was guaranteed to promote eyestrain from over-eager gazes attempting to probe over, around, and under those patches of enticing opacity.

Hoku's hair fell neatly down her back in a curtain of black, all the way to the beginning jut at the top of her pert backside. Both hair and backside also would draw longing gazes.

As Lizina studied her computrician, she understood why Chane had been attracted to this golden-skinned girl. Hoku, simply put, was sexy! Superlatively put, damned sexy!

"I have had it on for the past hour, trying to get used to it." Hoku shyly glanced up at her captain. "I have never been in public wearing anything so . . . so slight."

Lizina smiled. Hoku wasn't acting. She was genuinely embarrassed by the Webweave's revealing exposure.

"Then after we're through, you might save it for special occasions when you and Chane are alone." Lizina winked.

Hoku's grin conveyed that such was exactly her intention.

"Now, I need some help in getting ready for our . . . *entrance*."

Lizina pulled the smaller of two boxes from the

closet. She opened the lid to extract a strawberry blond wig. A thin plastic case lay at the bottom of the box. This she handed to Hoku, who opened it.

"A syringe?" Dark, liquid eyes widened.

"With enough subcutane dye to turn my skin six shades darker. I've never used one. I was hoping that you would do me the honor."

Hoku lifted the exodermic syringe from its plastic case. She turned it over in her small hand, eyeing it suspiciously.

"Captain, I've never even *seen* one of these before!"

Lizina cringed inwardly. "The instructions said to press the silvered end against arm or buttocks. It does the rest."

Hoku turned the syringe around so that the blunt, silvery-shining end pointed toward the ceiling. "Your arm?"

Lizina nodded and began rolling up the sleeve of her clingy, cream-colored blouse. She stopped with the cuff at her elbow and shook her head.

"The last time I took an injection in the arm it swelled and was sore for a week. I may need use of both arms tonight. You'd better administer the subcutane to the second option."

Peeling off her burgundy pants, Lizina bent over, hands on knees for support, and presented an unobstructed target for Hoku's ministration.

The Terasak walked rather apprehensively behind her captain. After a moment's hesitation, she firmly applied syringe to exposed rump.

There was a soft hiss as compressed air forced the dye through Lizina's skin and into her bloodstream, which would carry it to every cell in her body within thirty minutes. Lizina gritted her teeth and endured the sharp stinging sensation.

She stood and gingerly rubbed what felt to be a mortally wounded hindcheek. A knot had already begun to swell under the skin. She shook her head. While she might not be able to sit down for the next week—she would be able to use her arms!

Standing half naked before her computrician, Lizina saw no reason for feigning a modesty she did not possess. Grasping the bottom of her blouse, she pulled it over her head. She sensed Hoku's gaze on her as she took the second box from her closet. She smiled. Was the diminutive woman appraising her former competition for Chane's attentions?

The box contained Lizina's attire for the evening. In its own way, it was as provocative as Hoku's.

The two-piece SnugSuit (Tulann-designed, as was Hoku's Webweave) clung to Lizina's body like paint— black paint. The leotard-tight pants were delightfully highlighted by a series of open diamond-shaped panels that ran from ankle to waist. Elongated diamonds that exposed titillating glimpses of satiny flesh.

The diamond motif was continued on the sleeves of the blouse, which was equally, sexily black, and beneath the neckline of a high, flaring collar. The latter series of diamonds ran downward between Lizina's unhaltered breasts to stop at a wide belt, complete with a shining prass buckle, that encircled her slim waist.

Lizina completed her *haute couture* for the evening with spiked heels of gleaming jet equhyde. And the strawberry blond wig.

Maybe the wig was overdoing it, she mused. The point was, it remained exotic while disguising her own coppery hair. The gleaming, almost metallic hair was as rare as true blond among Galactics. It was hard to forget, as she had reason to know.

Kukis and Degula had held Lizina captive on *Forerunner* for a week. She had no doubt that were the two Chanks to see the hair again they would recognize it—and her. They had, after all, resurrected the embarrassing appellation, Coppertop.

An irrepressible shiver slithered up the length of her spine.

Coppertop!

She trembled, recalling the methods Kukis and Degula had used to bring back to life the woman she had once been.

First, they had used the Tingler. That insidiously modified mini-stopper Kukis carried.

A cold sweat prickled over Lizina's body at memory of the kiss of the Tingler's plexiplas barrel. Kukis's "toy" did not kill. It was designed specifically for the purpose of giving pain. Neuro-induced pain.

The nasty little device came complete with ten settings—each providing a geometric progression of agony!

Lizina had experienced only the first eight settings. That had been enough. Kukis had played his "toy" over her naked body while his First Mate had held her. Within minutes she had begged to service them; either and both of them.

The Tingler had not been enough for Kukis. It induced only *physical* pain. The captain of *Forerunner* had wanted to break her spirit, to remold her will.

He had. Within a cell black as his soul, and with a fine mist of skin-absorbed nightmare-breeding chemicals. For three days she had been in that awful cubicle. When she was at last released, she was no longer Lizina Harith, but Coppertop once again. A docile, subservient slave who existed only to provide sexual pleasures for others—those with the stells to buy her body.

Degula and Kukis paid nothing. They merely used me.

Tonight, if all went as scheduled, Lizina intended to repay the hospitality given her on *Forerunner*—with compounded interest. For her days of pain and anguish onboard the spacer, Kukis and Degula would know an eternity of the same.

An eternity of pain! And in the end—the far distant end—they will know total oblivion!

"Captain . . . Captain . . ." Hoku's voice filtered into Lizina's thoughts.

Lizina glanced to her computrician. Hoku stood beside the intercom grille. Willowy, clutched in her Webweave skintite; a vision of studiedly exotic erotica.

"Captain, it's Chane."

Nodding, Lizina moved to the grille. "Chane, Lizina here."

Tinny and dimensionless, *Windrammer*'s First Mate's voice answered, "Kukis and Degula have just entered the Hub Bar. Want me to stick with them?"

"No. Hoku and I will take it from here. Get back to the ship. Boldua is waiting for you." Lizina started to sign off, but added, "Chane . . . don't wait too long to take your positions. I don't relish actually having a romp with either Kukis or Degula."

"Pos! Soon as I pick up Boldua we'll take our positions. Just make certain you bring them down spoke-tunnel F-7."

"Will do." Lizina thumbed off the intercom.

She looked to Hoku. "We're on!"

The Hub Bar was small and dark. Of its twenty tables only four were occupied. A space station had little need of a bar. Greater pleasures lay a mere downlift to the planet itself. The Hub was for those unfortunate space-farers who were assigned to ship while the rest of their crewmates enjoyed the planet's varied diversions.

Later in the evening, the Hub would fill and the cyberbartenders would wheel and pivot among the packed tables. Now, the evening was young.

Lizina and Hoku paused at the entrance, allowing their eyes time to adjust to the interior darkness. Kukis and Degula were on the far side of the room, seated at the bar. (A real bar, low-slung and with swivel stools).

A shudder of revulsion—tinged with some dread—rippled through Lizina. And there was fear. Fear etched onto her psyche by those sessions on the wrong end of the Tingler. Fear imprinted on her brain by the cell of her detention and its chemical rain.

She fought that fear; she overcame it.

Lizina tilted her head toward the bar.

Hoku picked up the cue. "Jerra, I don't think we should be doing this. The Captain . . ."

"Vug, woman! The Captain's onplanet!" Lizina's voice was loud and brazen. "What she don't know won't hurt 'er. 'Sides, I'm tired of being penned up onboard. A woman's gotta get away from 'er work some time. Gotta get loose. Have some fun!"

They crossed the Hub and took two seats at the bar. Three vacant stools separated Lizina from Kukis. Another shudder ran through Lizina's body.

"Our Jarp-lovin' captain is a brother-spreadin' bitch!" Lizina waved to the cyberbartender. "Wasn't our rotation. Callah was supposed to stay with the ship!"

Kukis, who had sat talking with Degula, turned purposefully toward the loud woman . . . and his irritated expression transformed into a wide grin of surprise when his gaze fell on Lizina and her companion. His grin sparkled.

Lizina smiled. Her own gaze, lingering with implied interest, answered his. Damn fine job of acting, she admitted. She had forgotten how slimy Kukis was.

He was short, no more than a hundred-seventy sems. He wore black; shirt, trousers, and ever-shine, round-toed equhyde boots. The same style of attire he had worn while she had been captive onboard *Forerunner*. She fought back a shudder.

The sparkle in his grin came not from the Chank's overwhelming charisma, but from his teeth. Each was gold-rimmed with a small diamond inset at its center.

The woman beside him—Degula—wore red from toe

to neck. A simple form-fitting blouse and velveteen pants, snug.

Degula smiled while her gaze ran approvingly over Lizina and then Hoku. *Forerunner*'s First Mate had a decided taste for bed partners of the same sex.

The diamond-flashing grin and appraising smile led to the offer of a drink. Lizina and Hoku accepted, stool-sidling down beside Captain and Mate. And that drink led to another.

The cybernetic bartender made no judgments, no comments, and fair drinks.

By the time the third arrived, Kukis and Degula had less than subtly made their choices. Lizina sat beside Kukis. Not only did she endure his arm about her waist, she actually appeared to enjoy the hand that occasionally fondled her breast.

Hoku was beside Degula. The latter's hand rested in the computrician's lap. Fingers crept toward the Hoku's inner thigh, and upward.

Lizina silently applauded Hoku's acting ability. For a young woman—a girl, really!—who had been nervous about appearing in public clothed so scantily, the Terasak provided a convincing performance of a spacefarer on the make.

The bartender never brought a fourth round of drinks. By that time, Kukis and Degula had escorted the two willing cakes toward *Forerunner* where they would ably help pass the long lonely night. They took the most direct route . . . spoke-tunnel F-7.

Lizina scanned the cargo that lined each side of the corridor built into one of the space station's spokes. The stolen glances sought Chane and Boldua.

Her heart doubled the tempo of its beat. She didn't see them. Nor did her First Mate and DS officer make their presence known.

Now and then Hoku, who walked at Degula's side

ahead, half turned back to her. Lizina could see the
lines of worry that creased the young woman's forehead.

Lizina wasn't positive as to what thoughts were thread-
ing through Hoku's mind, but from her expression, they
were similar to those of her captain.

What if something has happened to Chane and Boldua?

The two were supposed to be waiting—hidden among
the cargo containers. They were to step out, stoppers in
hand, and rescue *Windrammer*'s captain and computrician
from a fate that was never worse than death.

Kukis reached the hatch to *Forerunner*, and neither
Chane nor Boldua had appeared.

Kukis placed his hand flat against the ship's palmlock.
The hatch slid open. The diamond-toothed captain turned
to Lizina. He waved an arm toward the open hatchway.

Hoku's eyes shifted to Lizina, wide and questioning.
So were her captain's.

Damn you, Chane! Where are you?

Lizina gave Hoku the most confident smile she could
summon, and stepped toward the hatch. If she were
going to get out of this—gracefully or not—she would
have to play it by ear. Perhaps once she was alone with
Kukis (an ice-floe moved along her spine at that pros-
pect) she could take his stopper. She had used a similar
trick to free herself of Mahir, back on Mirjam.

She silently cursed her decision to leave her own
stopper on *Windrammer*. The stoppers used by spacefarers here, in toward Galaxy Center lacked the modification common to pistols carried by whose who traveled
beyond the Carnadyne Void. The second setting only
jangled the nerves, with a bit more kick than the first
setting. Lizina's weapon's Two left its victim unconscious—as did Chane's. And that was the way she
wanted Kukis and Degula. At least for a while.

Lizina stepped into the ship. Horrible *deja vu* encompassed her. This was *Forerunner*. This was the ship that
had stolen her away from Panish and begun her months-

long nightmare. Her knees felt liquid and uneasy nausea washed through her stomach.

Taking a deep steadying breath, she turned to Hoku, who was following her through the hatchway. The yellowish caste to the computrician's face was three shades paler. Hoku was every bit as frightened as her captain.

Lizina glanced up to Kukis and Degula. Her heart trebled its pounding—in sheer relief!

Chane and Boldua stepped from among the packing crates. Without a sound, the two crept behind the pair of slavers and jabbed raised stoppers into their backs.

"One sound and you Fry!" Chane hissed through clenched teeth. "Inside and don't try anything stupid!"

"What is this? You can't . . ." Kukis stammered while his right hand dipped to the stopper strapped to his waist.

The cylinder in Chane's hand once more forcefully prodded the Chank's back. "Trying for the stopper would be stupid! Now, inside!"

Both Kukis and Degula moved their hands away from their weapons. Chane glanced up and winked at Lizina when he entered the ship. He slapped the hatch closed behind him.

"Sorry to cut it so close, Captain." Chane tossed Lizina a stopper. "But I was afraid if we moved any sooner someone might spot us."

Lizina flipped five. "As long as you arrived."

She trained the pistol on her two captives. A cold, humorless smile moved across her lips.

"Boldua, take their guns. Wouldn't want to give them the chance to make fools of themselves." When her DS officer had done as directed, Lizina turned to Chane. "You and Boldua give *Forerunner* a once over— on both levels. If any of the crew is onboard, zap them."

Boldua handed Hoku the confiscated stoppers and trotted off at Chane's side. By now Hoku had regained her color and smiled as coolly as Lizina. She aimed the weapons at Kukis and Degula.

"Jer . . . Captain, you've made a mistake. There's nothing onboard *Forerunner* of any value." Kukis's voice contained a quaver of fear. The same fear that widened his eyes.

"You're absolutely right. It's you two that I'm after." Lizina's smile widened.

She reached up to yank the ridiculous wig from her head. The long sleek cascade of her own hair tumbled downward about her shoulders.

"Coppertop!" The single gasp came from Degula.

Kukis's eyes merely widened to twice their size. His mouth moved, but nothing emerged.

"Captain Lizina Harith, *Windrammer*," Lizina corrected the First Mate. "A name, if I remember correctly, you once found unattractive. But one you'll never forget—throughout eternity!"

"Both levels clear!" Chane called as he and Boldua returned. "What shall we do with these two?"

"Take her to her cabin," Lizina said coldly with a tilt of her head to Degula, "and do with her as you please!"

Chane glanced at Hoku who visibly stiffened. When he looked back to Lizina, his expression said he would have no part of the Chank woman and what Lizina wanted done.

Lizina merely nodded and turned to Boldua (who eyed *Forerunner*'s First Mate with decided appreciation). "Boldua, she has no taste for men . . ."

"She'll have a taste of me before I'm through, Captain. And a mite more! It was a big Chank like this one they used for bait to get men onboard *Roundabout*. When I woke I was a slave on Panish." Boldua smiled at his captain. "I like 'em big!"

While Boldua (who was at least a head shorter than Degula) directed *Forerunner*'s First Mate to her cabin with a wave of his stopper, Lizina ordered Kukis in the opposite direction. Toward the spacer's con-cabin. Chane and Hoku followed.

Within the control room, one glance at Lizina's stopper setting—Three, to Fry—persuaded Kukis to open intership comm. He received clearance for *Forerunner*'s sudden and unexpected departure, no questions asked, in one hour.

Lizina then ordered Hoku and Chane to take the diamond-toothed captain to his room and leave him there. Bound and gagged on his bed. Naked.

When the three had departed the con-cabin, Lizina turned to the ship's curving console. She nodded. She saw only minor differences between it and *Windrammer*'s controls. She'd have no trouble piloting the craft.

She located intraship optics and flicked toggles until an image of Degula's room filled a holographic display to her left. She nodded her approval of the scene that met her gaze.

Boldua was giving Degula the promised taste of himself!

Both were naked. Lizina's DS officer stood above the kneeling woman. Good body on the man. His hands firmly grasped the back of her head, while his hips hunched with decided vigor. The ponderous length of his slicer sheathed and resheathed itself in the big woman's mouth. And, from the looks of it, Lizina saw with approval, several sems deeper than that. Degula snuffled and spluttered.

"Lizina," Chane's voice came from behind her.

She swiveled around.

Chane held out the two tinglers Lizina had special-ordered from a Panish gunsmith. She accepted the mini-stoppers; she accepted the cassette Chane took from his pocket. Its duplicate cassette was onboard *Windrammer*.

"Better redshift. You need to get clearance for *Windrammer*. I don't want to make this jaunt alone."

Chane smiled. "I'll be right at your side, Captain. I have no intention of losing you now. Not when you're so close to closing out all your accounts."

"Everything paid in full—in a few more hours," she mused aloud as she watched Chane leave the con-cabin.

Hoku awaited her man outside. The golden-skinned woman slipped an arm about Chane's waist, hugging him tightly with obvious relief. *Windrammer*'s First Mate returned the greeting before the couple moved on down the tunnel.

Lizina swiveled back to the holographic display. Boldua could have his pleasure with Degula for another forty minutes. After that it was time to begin the First Mate's (and her captain's) final voyage along the spaceways!

18

Gravity: it attracts and holds.

For eons the well it formed about a barely remembered planet called Homeworld (once Earth, now Urth) confined humankind to the surface of that world. It was the invisible, unbreakable chain that bound a young race to a ball of clay while the stars of the galaxy winked seductively in the heavens.

Nuclear force—strong interaction.

Nuclear force—weak interaction.

Electromagnetic force.

Gravitational force.

Thus were listed the four physical forces that bound the firmament. The four prime forces of the universe, in descending order of strength.

The first two had to be measured by their effects over distances so minute that they were non-distances to the unaided human eye. The third, electromagnetism, encompassed the full spectrum of light and beyond, at both ends. From X rays to the ultraviolet; from ultraviolet to heat.

The fourth was gravity, and it was the least of them all.

So weak was its force that for decades it was a source of controversy among the scientists of Homeworld. Was gravity an actual force at all, or was it rather an *effect*; the observable effect of some other phenomenon?

The gravity waves that had been theorized by those

primitive physicists continued undetectable until the early Twenty-second century (Old Style). Soon thereafter came GUT: the Grand Unified Theory. The long-sought unified field theory that described the universe in one compact and neatly defined equation. Even with GUT, any description for laymen of the physical workings of matter and energy continued to be divided into four categories.

And the weakest force in the universe was gravity.

Gravity! The power that held planets in their orbits. The force that locked civilizations, whether human or otherwise, to the surface of their worlds. The power that crumbled great mountains and artificially constructed walls.

The weakest force in the universe!

Yet the opposite appeared to be the case. Of those four mighty forces that comprised and ruled the galaxy, gravity was the most observable. That is, its effects were; gravity made apples fall, towers lean, aircraft plummet from the sky, basketballs drop through hoops and force their way through dangling nets, sliders dip as they zipped over home plate, legs and backs break when fragile humans slipped from ladders.

All of that was clearly observable, whereas atoms and a great deal of the effect of electromagnetism were not. Yet here physics agreed with that philosophy that stated things were not as they seemed. In fancier terms, observability and strength did not equate.

To defy gravity!

It was a dream, an ambition; the dream of humankind for eons.

In pursuit of that goal Icarus and Daedalus sought escape through flight and their race built balloons and gliders and eventually heavier-than-air machines that allowed brief leaps from the surface of Homeworld. And so, envying birds, those thingmakers of old Urth came to construct towering chemical rockets that thrust their kind up from the binding surface of its world.

Upward into space, past the birds and the clouds, by sheer brute force! Free of the confining gravity that had held them as if in the bottom of a well! Gravity defied—and overcome after millions of years!

(Few considered that humankind had always held the power to defy gravity. The weakest of human infants accomplished the feat at the moment of birth, merely by lifting the smallest of its delicate fingers.)

The weakest of forces, then. Gravity.

And yet from that force, the most insignificant of those that forever bound matter and energy, came the very devourer of the universe!

The Maelstrom.

It reigned as malign monarch of the star-crowded center of the galaxy. A nothingness . . . with a gravitational force beyond imagining.

Humankind had known of The Maelstrom since the race first ventured in, in toward galaxy center. It was called the Farther Reaches then, because it was far and far from Homeworld, out on the whip-like outer arm of the spiral galaxy . . . which was of course the galaxy's real Farther Reaches. Across twenty-seven thousand light-years lumbered the first spaceships, and threaded their way amid that brilliant splash of stars living and dead, to discover The Maelstrom.

That devourer of space and matter was the subject of countless monographs and debates filled with theories. The Maelstrom was also the center of an equally endless number of scientific research projects that spanned those same centuries.

There continued a notable lack of any extensive knowledge of that deepest of gravity wells, at Galaxy Center.

Oh, it had been a star, of course. A great flaming hydrogen furnace of a sun that had lived and died in a spectacularly flaring supernova long before the evolutionary ancestors of *Homo sapiens* crawled on their fins from swampy mire.

"It merely got too big for its britches," a famous scientist had said, to be quoted, "and consumed itself. Like the punctured ego of some of my mistaken colleagues, it fell in on itself."

The burned-out core of that supernova was big, bigger than big, bigger than two and a half live solar masses—the limit for a peaceful sun-death. The star that once existed where The Maelstrom now yawned had indeed collapsed. Its own core pulled it in. That super-dense core fell in on itself. Matter compressed, compacted. In turn, it collapsed anew and was compressed.

Smaller and smaller the core pressed, folding inward until there was . . . nothing. A nothingness. And yet that was impossible.

"A ball of aluminum foil the size of your head might weigh a kilo," Lizina had once been told. "Crush it until it is the size of a marble and it still weighs a kilo. It will seem heavier, though, because it is so small. Crush it into invisible nothingness, if that were possible for a ball of foil, and it will still weigh that same kilo."

The great star at the center of the galaxy no longer existed. It was a dead star, a collapstar. Gravity had tugged and pulled and forced and shrunk the core into nothingness. And still it retained its mass, and every iota of its gravitic power.

It had become The Maelstrom. A collapstar; a black hole. The ultimate gravitic force. And there it lurked like a spider; like an octopus patiently awaiting the approach of prey to feed it.

The Maelstrom. A bottomless gravity well that sucked "real" space into oblivion. Gravity so concentrated, so mighty that not even light could escape. Light strove to rush from that grasping nothingness at 300,000 kilometers per second—and could not achieve escape velocity from the incredible pull of The Maelstrom!

Without light, The Maelstrom became a trapdoor spider. It could not be seen. It was an apparent nothingness in space. An eerie absence of light, of *anything*. The ultimate absence of light was the ultimate black. It was not a hole in space, but it appeared to be, and it was called a "black hole" just the same.

Anything, whether particle of space-dust or chunk of rock or planetary body or comet, caught in the Maelstrom's grasp was sucked into that devouring maw. Time itself was twisted during that last plunging journey. To an observer out beyond the pull of The Maelstrom, the plunging victim never completed its fall. Magic seemed to supervene. So warped was the abstract concept that humankind called "time" that it appeared to stop—completely, totally!

A plunge into a collapstar took an eternity.

And there was no return.

No one knew The Maelstrom's original size, nor would anyone ever know. This most immense of what had been mis-called "black holes" had existed before humankind was humankind. The Maelstrom's pull exceeded the speed of light, and that force—that event horizon—extended farther than any other. It extended a thousand kloms.

Once there had been a star bigger than big . . .

It was here that Lizina brought *Forerunner,* with Boldua tensely at SIPACUM. Now the ship hung motionless in space a hundred thousand kloms from the collapstar's event horizon.

Lizina's fingers tapped at glow-green buttons and maneuvering rockets ignited. Telits flashed. The spacer's prow swung gently about to point directly into the open throat of oblivion.

She stared at the gravity grid that SIPACUM drew on a monitor to her right, and she smiled. The high resolution image graphically depicted what was *not* there—in "real" space. The Maelstrom's event horizon; that point beyond which even racing light itself could no longer escape the ever-increasing pull of gravity.

Lizina stared, fascinated and mystified, at the optical scan of The Maelstrom. She saw nothing.

Boosted in infrared, a thin red line could be seen encircling the nothingness. The red circle was formed by traces of particles in decay as they were sucked beyond the event horizon—redshifted into oblivion.

Into The Maelstrom, forever.

She stared at the complete absence of light, and she shivered.

There were those who theorized that tachyons, with their infinite velocity, could in fact escape a collapstar's bottomless gravity well. Even The Maelstrom's. That remained theory. No one had been so foolish as to take a spacer into the mouth of absolute nothingness and then attempt tachyon conversion: attempt to jump free in the faster-than-light nonentity of "subspace." If such a situation had occurred accidentally, it was assumed to be a failure. There existed none along the spaceways who claimed success in such a reckless venture, and none who cared to try.

Nor was Lizina here to further scientific research. The victim become manhuntress was completing her vengeance, while incidentally ridding the spaceways of some of its slimiest prowlers.

Boldua glanced over from his SIPACUM interface. "Captain: *Windrammer* should blueshift in ten minutes."

"Disable the tachyon converter. Set the drive for self-disabling in—whatever time SIPACUM says is sufficient. Then prepare to receive the S-tunnel from *Windrammer*." She spoke with lips tight, and pushed from her chair before the console. She stood with a tingler in each hand. "I have other matters to attend to."

Boldua nodded as she left the con-cabin, a tigress on the prowl. He did not ask the specifics of those "other matters." He tried not even to think.

* * *

Kukis's head twisted toward Lizina when she entered the cabin. His eyes were wide and frightened. His nostrils flared. Muffled words came from behind the gag crammed in his mouth. He strained at the polyrope that bound him spread-eagled on his bed.

Lizina considered the gag and decided to leave it in place. She had no desire to endure his curses—or his screams.

Moving beside the bed, she stared down at the man who had so abused her mind and body. She told him of *Forerunner*'s position and the trajectory she had planned for the vessel. Straight into the yawning mouth of the Maelstrom.

Lizina held high one of the tinglers for Kukis's examination. The swine's eyes were pools of terror, filled with the realization of what she intended to do before sending *Forerunner* on its final journey.

"I wish I had the time to return all the courtesy you provided during my brief stay onboard this ship." Her voice was cold and hard, devoid of emotion. "But circumstances do not allow the opportunity to demonstrate fully the pleasures of your cell and its chemical mists. All I have time for is this."

She lowered the plexiplas rod to Kukis's belly and squeezed the handle. The man merely glared up at her.

The tingler was on its first setting. Its bite was that of a mild electrical shock, a paper cut, and an annoying sting of a mosquito melted together. Lizina knew. Kukis had delighted in introducing her naked body to the tingler.

The second of the nasty little device's settings was similar to One: double voltage, bee sting, and a shallow razor cut rolled into one. Painful, but bearable.

Lizina ignored the second setting. She twisted the silvered ring at the base of the tingler's handle to Three.

As Kukis had done to her, she lightly brushed his cheek and squeezed. He twitched and squirmed, throwing his weight against the polyrope. The bindings held him securely atop the bed.

Three squared the sensations of the second setting—and added heat.

Languidly, Lizina ran the rod over his lips, across his hairless chest and belly. She stopped when she had twice encircled his penis and balls. Her only regret was that she could not plunge the hard rod into his body as he had done to her.

If I had told Chane to tie him face down . . .

She edged the thought away. There was no time to rearrange *Forerunner*'s captain now. Only time enough to give him a sample of the pain he had delighted in providing her.

"Four!" She twisted the ring, then twisted it again. "Five!"

She recalled the geometric progression of agony each new setting brought. And she smiled as she retraced the invisible, serpentine trail that ran from Kukis's cheek to his hairless crotch.

The bound man writhed. Sweat beaded his forehead. Muffled cries of anguish fought their way through the gag stuffed in his mouth.

By the time Eight had reached his vulnerably exposed genitals, his body convulsed.

Lizina paid him no heed. She twisted the silver ring to Ten and once more applied the plexiplas rod. When she had completed the leisurely course downward, she shoved the tingler beneath the bound man.

Kukis's back arched high and rigid. He held himself there. He had to, had to. The tingler remained under him.

Lizina nodded silent approval. Eventually his muscles would tire and his body would slowly lower to the device again. His own weight would be enough to trip the firing mechanism in the handle. Yet another jolt of setting Ten would slice through his nerve endings.

So it would be for eternity—as *Forerunner* fell into the Maelstrom and time slowed to a standstill. When her children's children held great-grandchildren on their knees, Kukis's back would still be arching in a desperate struggle to escape the Tingler.

Lizina left him there and walked from the cabin to Degula's quarters. The same fate awaited *Forerunner*'s First Mate.

Inserting the cassette that had brought *Forerunner* to the Maelstrom, Lizina's fingertips commanded SIPACUM to erase and degauss the tiny crystal held within the rectangle of plastic. A moment later SIPACUM announced that the former tetradecimal commands no longer existed and the crystal was ready for reuse.

Again Lizina's fingers moved over SIPACUM's keyboard. This time she encoded a simple program. Ten minutes after loading into the processing and computing unit, the program would run. Its sole function was to fire the maneuvering rockets while maintaining a trajectory straight into the Maelstrom.

With the program saved to crystal, Lizina pulled the cassette from SIPACUM and hefted it in her palm. Should Kukis and Degula somehow manage to shed the polyrope binding them (highly improbable, though not impossible), they would still be totally helpless.

Boldua had virtually destroyed *Forerunner*'s drive. And this cassette would drain the maneuvering rockets. The ship had no other form of propulsion.

Once started on its voyage into the Maelstrom, the spacer would continue until it reached the surface of the collapstar—which was theoretically impossible since the star no longer existed.

"Captain," Boldua's voice came from the grille on

the con, ''the S-tunnel is secure. Chane is ready for us to come onboard *Windrammer*.''

Lizina turned to the con. ''I'll be right down.''

She swiveled back to SIPACUM and inslotted the cassette. With an almost affectionate pat to the side of the computing unit, she rose and paced from *Forerunner*'s con-cabin.

No one spoke. Instead they silently counted off the remaining minute while their gazes were as if magnetically grappled to the holographic display.

Four orange-red blossoms bloomed from *Forerunner*'s stern. The ship, momentum overcome, slipped forward, away from *Windrammer*. Forward into the black throat of eternity.

Lizina hit a toggle to kill the optic display. She had seen enough. Until the day she died, all she need do was glance to the stars and know that the voyage Kukis and Degula had just begun still continued. That the two still suffered for the agony they had inflicted on her mind and body.

''Hoku, inslot the Panish cassette.'' Lizina nodded to her computrician. ''It's time to take *Windrammer* home!''

19

Shielding her dark eyes with a hand, Ganesa of Resh glanced upward. The sun that hung overhead was pale yellow, big, and unrelentingly hot. The first two attributes were insignificant to her. The last was worse than irritating.

The Diamond Lady of the spaceways felt most unladylike. The black body stocking she wore, soggy with sweat, clung to the feminine contours of her body. It chafed. Sweat, too, had destroyed the curled coiffure of her flaming red hair. It was plastered against her skull like a greasy cap of wet and matted string. She cursed under her breath, employing the profanities of five different languages. None fully expressed the contempt she felt for this unknown world or the situation that had ensnared her.

Oh sure, the grisly god Gri had saved her, and four of *Be Lively*'s crew. (The others lay dead, necks broken during the tumultuous atmospheric entry and landing). For what purpose? Had He protected her body and soul only to prolong her suffering and agony? Did the blood-thirsty god of Resh derive unholy pleasure from watching her slowly die on this blast furnace of a world?

Gri's black heart!

Ganesa wiped ineffectually at the rivulets of sweat that trickled down her forehead toward her squinted eyes while she peered over the flatness that surrounded her belly-landed ship. A never-ceasing wind blew across the grassy plain to lick hotly at her face. Waist-high blades of green rippled like emerald water that rolled up to engulf her. Stretching endlessly on all sides was the monotonous green, and the flatness.

With a grunt of disgust, Ganesa turned back to the gargantuan dome of gleaming naked metal that was *Be Lively*. Grudgingly she admitted that the unobstructed plain had played no small part in the ship's successful landing. *Be Lively* was a spacer, not an in-gravity boat. Its designers had never intended that the ship suffer the rigors of atmospheric flight or the brutal contact of hull to earth.

But the space-traveling brothel had survived its plummeting planetfall. With a scratch-built computer that was a notch above a calculator and years upon years of experience at *Be Lively*'s control console, Ganesa had managed to bring her ship safely onto this Gri-forsaken plain.

Trying to ignore the hollowness of futility that leeched at the seed of hope she desperately clung to, she began to circle the ship. Again. For the fourth time. The first three times Ganesa had found no signs of serious damage to the hull.

Oh there were dents—big ones. But no jagged rips marred the spacer's skin, or even noticeable holes. The hull would have to be triple-checked sem by square sem. They had to be absolutely certain no minute rent in the metal existed before any attempt was made to move *Be Lively*.

Yet as best as Ganesa could judge, her precious spacer remained intact. A bit battered, oh yes, but capable of slicing its way across the lightyears of the spaceways.

If—if—there existed a method of getting the ship offplanet and leaping free of its gravitational pull.

The "if" was a tremendous obstacle. But then, so had been bringing the spacer in safely. She had managed that. Given time, she would get *Be Lively* back to space. Or her crew would die trying.

"Captain!" The voice called from her left.

Ganesa turned. Fordel, her DS officer, waded through the wind-rippled grass with the three remaining crew-members at his side. For ten minutes the four men had searched the general area surrounding *Be Lively*. Ganesa was uncertain what they had expected to find, but it had kept them occupied and given her time to ponder seemingly insurmountable obstacles that stood between her and the vastness of space.

"We won't starve to death here!" Fordel held up a limp rust-furred creature that appeared to be a rabbit, minus the long ears. "Got it with my stopper!"

Ganesa did her best to smile. Starving was the last concern plaguing her mind. *Be Lively* was fully stocked and vegetables could be cloned. If starvation were to be a problem, it lay years ahead.

"Should I skin it for dinner?" Fordel's toothy grin spread across his dark face with obvious manly pride in his prowess.

Civilized man reverted to primitive hunter! Ganesa grimaced. That the creature might be poisonous had apparently never entered the man's thoughts. His grin drooped when she explained what should have been obvious even to the greenest of spacefarers stranded on an unknown world.

"SIPACUM could run an analys . . ." Fordel's words and revived grin faded with the realization that SIPACUM was dead.

Ganesa shook her head and began circling the ship again. How could she expect to escape this world with men such as Fordel aiding her? Did she really believe there was a way to escape this hellhole of a planet?

Yes! Dammit! Yes!

She had to believe that the means to raise *Be Lively* back to the stars existed. If she didn't, it would be easier to set a stopper on Three, point it at her temple, and squeeze the handle. She nurtured no illusions about the freedoms and pleasures of living on a primitive planet. The "return to nature" philosophy that periodically infected the minds of Galactics left much to be desired. Ganesa of Resh was unashamedly a worshipper of *things* concocted by a race of thingmakers. Without the luxury provided by those things there could be no living, only existing. A quick clean death would be much better than slowly rotting away on this inferno of a world.

Much better!

Ganesa had no intention either of rotting away or putting a stopper to her head. She would find a way to get off this . . .

A stopper hummed, behind her.

Ganesa whirled. And froze. Her brain refused to accept the image transmitted by her eyes!

The image was real, horribly real.

Fordel stood where she had left him. His right arm was extended, directing the almost invisible beam of his stopper at an . . . an insect . . . that rushed head-on toward the man!

On four legs!

The creature's uppermost pair of legs was outstretched toward Fordel. Each of the jointed appendages ended in a wickedly pointed, scythelike recurved claw.

The insect thing—fully two meters in length—barreled forward on legs that pumped like pistons driven by some engine gone out of control. Neither the dense grass nor the sonic beam hampered its charge. The gleaming blue-black chitin covering its body with armor-plate protection afforded the grotesque monster the same shielding against sonic weapons that a spacesuit gave its wearer.

Its heavy triangular head wove from side to side. The

mandibles of its mouth—two insidiously pointed hooks—gnashed together, then opened wide.

Ganesa had never seen . . .

No!

She *had* seen the creature before. On her homeworld Resh! Children there often tied strings about black-horned beetles, then pitted the bugs in mortal combat. But those insects grew to no more than a sem in length. This monster was fully two meters!

And it was atop Fordel!

One of the great clawed arms slashed out. The DS officer screamed. His hand—still gripping the handle of the stopper—flew through the air. A fountain of red spewed from the raw stub of his wrist.

The creature's other arm swept upward in a tight arc. A needle-pointed claw knifed into the DS officer's abdomen just below his rib cage. An instant later the recurved tip appeared again—protruding from Fordel's throat.

The man's scream dwindled to a piteous gurgle. Then he was silent.

Like a woman awakening from a nightmare, Ganesa dropped her right hand to the stopper strapped to her waist. Her fingers never closed about the handle.

Three spikelike spears jabbed at her stomach. High-pitched, threatening chirps filled her head. Ganesa froze once more. This time in sheer terror. She sucked in a deep breath, and another, to steady herself.

Twenty gigantic insects had followed the blue-black killer from the high grass. Each bore the spike-spears.

Metal? She wasn't certain. They held them in lobster-like jammer claws. Every one of the needle-honed weapons was aimed at the four remaining survivors of *Be Lively.*

Like Fordel's monstrous killer, each of the grotesque creatures moved on its four hind legs while using its prothoractic pair as "arms." The twenty armed insectoids, however, were at least half a meter shorter than the blue-black giant.

"Booda!" The cry of horror burst from the throat of *Be Lively*'s computrician. "Save us!"

Ganesa's head twisted to the source of the cry. What she saw was the gargantuan terror lifting Fordel's corpse, still skewered like a side of meat on that single razor-sharp claw, into the air. It accomplished the task as though Fordel's dead weight were no more than a kilo or two.

The creature's free claw probed at the limp, lifeless body. Like a skinner's blade opening the belly of a fur-bearing animal, the claw drove inward and sliced downward.

Ganesa's head jerked away. Even so she was not quick enough. That one glimpsed moment remained etched in her brain. She would see it in her nightmares for the rest of her life—Fordel's stomach opening and his entrails coiling outward.

She heard one of her crew members retch. The sound set her own stomach aquiver with uneasy spasms that grew to quaking nausea. Forgetting the spikes that prodded her, she doubled over and emptied her stomach. She remained that way until only dry heaves wracked her trembling body.

Clutching her belly, she waited until her strength slowly returned. When she rose, it was with her hand about her stopper. She wrenched the pistol free of its holster. Her thumb flicked the setting to Three.

The sonic beam seemed merely to irritate Fordel's killer. Still, that was all she needed. Irritation. A moment's confusion. If she could achieve that, she could run. *Be Lively*'s hatch was only fifty meters away, around the curve of the ship.

Inside the DS! And that could be manually operated.

No living creature known to Galactics could withstand a plasma bolt. She was willing to risk her life on the chance that these monsters' chitinous shells would not protect them from a searing blast of raw energy.

Ganesa never managed to aim her pistol.

A hammer she never saw slammed into the side of her head. She staggered one step and half turned. Aswirl in a blur of pain-tears, she saw that Fordel's killer hovered above her. The horned triangle of its head sat askew on a thin neck as though thoroughly perplexed by the soft-bodied creature swaying before it.

In the next instant, Ganesa felt her knees go liquid. She tumbled face forward into the blackness that leaped up to engulf her. Her last coherent thought was a praise to Gri for bringing unconsciousness. If the monster were going to kill her, at least she would be spared the pain.

Genesa did not die. She awoke with a pounding headache whose spikes of pain radiated from an egg-sized lump on the side of her head.

She also awoke to find the remnants of her body stocking in shreds. Both warheads and her stash felt bruised. There was justification for the tenderness. Her computrician related how the blue-black killer had carefully torn away her clothing, then thoroughly probed breasts and pubis while she lay unconscious.

"It was as though it saw the difference in you and us," the man said. His head tilted toward his companions, then he looked down at himself. All three were as naked as Ganesa. "He fondled all of us. Gods, Captain! The damned thing thinks! You can see it if you watch him."

Ganesa's gaze rose to the insect monster that sat back on metathorax legs and abdomen ten meters away. Its multi-faceted eyes shifted back and forth, then froze to stare at the lone woman as though noting Ganesa's return to consciousness.

Its mandibles clicked sharply three times. Then twice.

The clicks were followed by a series of high-pitched chirps from the fluttering palps of its mouth.

Two of the spearbearers surrounding Ganesa and crew moved forward. One reached out to clasp Ganesa's right arm. With steadily increasing pressure from the pincer claw, it forced her to her feet. The second repeated the procedure with the computrician.

Jerking man and woman about so that they faced each other, the spearbearers shoved captain and subordinate together and held them there with one "arm." The insects' other armlike appendages stroked the genitals of their captives.

Ganesa shivered at the repulsive touch of intimacy. She gritted her teeth and bore the humiliation. If she were to survive, she had no other recourse.

After what seemed an eternity of nerve-grating degradation, the stroking stopped. The insects' heads tilted from side to side while multi-celled eyes studied woman and man. The moment of reprise was short-lived. The jammer claws clamped tighter, threatening to break vulnerably frail human skin, and thrust the captives together again.

"I think . . . I believe . . . they want . . ." the computrician stammered. He glanced to his denuded loins and the limp slicer asleep there. "I can't!"

Ganesa, seething with disgust and contempt, glared at the man. Was her deep-seated distaste for him? Or for the act the blue-black killer obviously wanted to see performed?

Again the pincer tightened on her arm and once more she was shoved rudely against the computrician's nakedness.

The man stared at her. His eyes pleaded as loudly as his voice. "I can't. Not here. Not like this!"

"The hell you can't! If I can—you can! It's our lives, you fool!"

Still in the grip of her spearbearer, Ganesa sank to her

knees at the man's feet. With her lips open wide, she leaned forward and took him into her mouth.

The computrician could, and did. So did the other two members of her crew, before night ended their first day on the uncharted world.

On the morning of the second day, Ganesa and crew were bound together with woven ropes of grass that withstood all attempts to break them. Equally surprising was that the insects had apparently constructed them while Ganesa and her crew slept.

The captives' hands were tied behind their backs while a long rope was looped about each of their necks. In single file, led by one spearbearer with rope in claw and with spearbearers to each side, they walked. They walked all day.

The trek through the high grass was westward, as best as Ganesa could judge. And it was long. The blue-black killer, which she realized was the band's leader, never stopped. If either she or a member of her crew slowed the pace, all were prodded onward with the tip of a spear pointedly applied to their bare backsides or thighs.

Only when that boiling horror of a sun sank and the planet's three moons rose did the band stop.

As it had done the evening before, the leader sat back and watched while Ganesa lay on her back and spread for her three crew members. Again she endured.

That night Ganesa slept little. Instead she lay naked in the grass, resting her aching muscles—and watching.

Her insect captors did sleep—in shifts (two hours each, she estimated). Even the Leader curled its six legs beneath its thorax and nestled in the grass while four of the spearbearers stood guard around the resting creature.

She had no doubt the monsters (if they bore a name, she had discerned no indication of it) were semi-sentient if not fully reasoning entities. The clicks of their hooked mandibles, the chirps, the motion of their antennae, the waves of their arm-legs were unmistakably a language. How complex or abstract in nature was the system of insect communication, she had no method of determining.

And they carried weapons. The spike-spears constituted tools. That indicated an intelligence exceeding the usual communal mind Galactics associated with advanced insect species.

Their reason for capturing her and the members of her crew, however, lay beyond Ganesa. The Leader and his troops (she thought of them as a military unit just as for some reason she thought of the Leader as he) had given no indication as to why they had taken four human prisoners. Other, of course, than to provide voyeuristic entertainment for the Leader each evening.

The answer to that came two days later. Two long, burning days with no food and only occasional stops at the rare streams that snaked shallowly through the plain.

That answer was twofold: the city and the forest.

The city consisted of ten ziggurat-like pyramids. Great mounds of sun-baked bricks. Each side measured a klom and from base to flat top soared almost a klom. Insect mounds! Colonies for Ganesa's gigantic beetle-like captors. The monsters swarmed to and from the mounds in neatly ordered lines. Millions of the creatures.

And their slaves!

Ganesa noted that at least three other gargantuan insect species marched in the endless lines. Spearbearers were positioned along the lines to assure their continual orderly movement, and to quell any thought of escape. Assuming that these monsters did indeed think.

Slaves—to bugs!

Any thought—or hope—Ganesa held that this would not be her fate was crushed. She and her crew were led to the nearest line of insects that plodded into the forest. Their hands were untied and their buttocks prodded.

They scurried forward to keep pace with the flowing file. Into the forest they scuttled.

There other insects worked among the trees, harvesting orange melonlike fruits from the limbs. Ganesa's arms were filled with the fruits and she hastened back to the mound city to deposit the burden in a lofty storage room within one of the ziggurats.

Like an infinite loop, the process began anew. Ganesa, a human insect among a file of alien bugs, half-walked half-trotted back to the forest. Then to the city, arms laden with the orange melons, merely to return to the trees for yet another load . . .

Only when night came were she and her crew herded into a sprawling hard-mud large room crowded with other slaves—insects! They were given three of the (edible but tasteless) orange fruits and Ganesa was once again bred. Yes, bred. Now she realized that voyeurism had nothing to do with the nightly servicing of her crew; she was female and females produced new slaves.

In the morning, there were the lines, and the head, and the forest.

The next night was a repeat of the one before. The following morning a duplicate of its predecessor. By the end of the first month Ganesa no longer thought of the spaceship only three days to the east, slowly disappearing into the vegetation. That made her existence easier. She even found herself enjoying the three men, the three stinking men, their hair matted, who used her body each night. After all, they provided some pleasure and they did break the tedium of the harvest—and they were human!

20

The lift to Qalaraport from Norcross came with all the joyous celebration of a funeral. *Misfit*'s crew simply sat and stared morbidly at the floor, out the viewports, at each other, while the elevator rose, toward the space station in orbit above Qalara's capital city.

No one spoke. Not even Varnalgeran Yuw, who had spent the past two days carefully selecting his promised wardrobe. (A portion of which he now wore—a bibbed shirt in eye-blinding purple, with prass buttons, matching pants, and a new white Wayne banded with feathers and beads.)

The reason for their shared gloom was Songan.

Upon planetfall, *Misfit*'s First Mate had disappeared for two days. He had reappeared to accompany his companions back to the ship. One glance at the drawn aspect of his nut-brown subcutaned face had told them everything.

The journey to Qalara had been fruitless.

No one asked any questions. When Songan was ready to discuss what he had learned at Hakimit Med Center, he would. Until then, he would carry it within him. Meanwhile he would perform his tasks with total efficiency. This was the way of Songan of Harb. Comfort—when and if it came—came from within. That was the way of the Tao, and Songan was the consummate Taoist.

An hour after boarding *Misfit* (under the Lanatian registry *Waystar*), Dorjan received clearance to embark.

Another thirty minutes passed before SIPACUM punched the spacer into subspace—coalesced tachyons streaming across the Farther Reaches toward Panish—toward Lizina!

Dorjan toed open intraship comm. "Standard conwatch rotation. Songan has first shift. The rest of you are on free time. Time I suggest would be well spent in catching up on lost sleep!"

The two days on Qalara had not all been spent shopping for Yuw's outrageous clothing. Both captain and crew had sampled more than ample portions of the various wines and liquors for which Qalara was known throughout the galaxy. (All excellent, Dorjan admitted, though Qalara's beers were lacking in comparison to Thebanis's Starflare).

Sampled, too, had been Qalara's equally delightful women (and men—Songbird had no sexual preference; just a Jarp's sexual appetite).

The two days onplanet had been good. A well-deserved mini-vacation for captain and crew. Good for all onboard, except the First Mate.

Dorjan studied his friend from the corner of an eye, then turned to Varn and tilted his head toward the door. The computrician pushed from his chair at SIPACUM without question and redshifted.

Dorjan swiveled to his fellow Harbian. He took a deep breath.

"Care to get it off your chest?"

Songan's shaven head turned from the control console.

"There's nothing to say . . . not really. Hakimit can't do anything. Even if they wanted to."

"Can't?" Dorjan stared at his friend uncertain what he meant.

"It was a waste of time, Dorjan." Songan leaned back in the conformachair. His eyes were without luster. "Hakimit Med apparently does human cloning. Getting them to admit to that was a major task in itself! They don't like to talk about the 'internal operations' of Hakimit."

He paused for a heavy, silent moment. "I did manage to talk with one daktari. She was tight-lipped but confirmed that Hakimit does 'participate' in 'certain cloning projects' involving human subjects. Exactly what those projects were, she refused to say.

"She did say—in convoluted terms—that only the very rich and very powerful of Qalara were involved." Songan shrugged. "She made it plain that my case— Yoluta—does not qualify for the program."

Dorjan felt rage slowly mounting within him. Songan was his friend, and no one, especially not some administrator securely insulated by bureaucratic mumbo-jumbo, had the right to say a friend was unqualified.

"We can get stells—take them from Qalara, if need be."

Songan shook his head. "She was emphatic about the program being closed. Stells aren't enough to unlock Hakimit's secrets."

Again Songan sat silently. His gaze moved over the con with its colorfully flashing lights and displays.

"Dorjan, she explained that cloning isn't enough to bring Yoluta back. The body could be cloned, yes . . . but not the mind. A cloned brain is like a—a blank cassette. It has to be encoded, imprinted."

He looked at Dorjan. "Apparently Hakimit requires a brain scan from each of its special clients. The scans provide the needed information to imprint the clone. The scan *is* the individual—personality, memory, conscious and unconscious. The scans have to be updated periodically to keep the subject's memories current."

Dorjan glanced at the floor. A body was merely a shell. Yoluta, the woman Songan had loved—still loved— was more than a body. It was beyond Hakimit's ability to bring Yoluta back to his friend.

"The daktari mentioned one other possibility," Songan said, his voice weary. "There's new research in progress out on Hawking."

"Hawking?" Dorjan's head jerked up.

The planet was the outermost of Galactic worlds, hanging away out there on the rim, the spiral arm of the galaxy. It was considered the cultural hub of human civilization. Neither he nor Songan had been to Hawking.

"I'm not certain if it's worth considering. It is a completely new avenue—memory imprinting on a cellular level. The researchers have theorized that the DNA in each human cell contains a chemo-electrical code of each individual's long-term and executive memories."

The research sounded farfetched to Dorjan. *But so did faster-than-light travel to my ancestors,* he mused, trying hopelessly to be hopeful.

"Do you want to try a jaunt to Hawking?" Dorjan used the term "jaunt" loosely. Hawking was half a galaxy from what was called the Farther Reaches. Hawking *was* the Farther Reaches. Its sun had been named Centaur, once.

Songan shook his head. "The research is only in its seminal stages. Nothing conclusive has been proven to demonstrate that there is any validity to the theory. I think it's time I buried my dead and started looking to the future."

"The Kuzih planets?"

Songan nodded without enthusiasm. "But first I have to get my captain to Panish! There's a woman waiting for him there."

Dorjan reached out and squeezed his friend's shoulder. He smiled as best he could. "If you need to talk more, you know where my cabin is."

The gentle giant nodded and turned back to the con.

Dorjan left him there to sort through his memories and find a way to bury a woman whose life and love had been treacherously stolen from him.

21

Lizina received the invitation from a Captain Nibaw of the Suzite spacer *Suzi City Slinger* to meet him onboard the ship. The object was to discuss *Windrammer*'s relieving Nibaw of two holds full of calculator parts destined for Shankar. Lizina was interested in the cargo, but not the meeting place.

Nibaw (over intership comm) chuckled at her "unwarranted caution" and agreed to meet her in Panishport's Hub Bar to discuss the transaction.

Half an hour later, Lizina was in tears. She was also in the arms of "Captain Nibaw," smothering him with kisses and doing her damnedest to squeeze the air out of his lungs.

The tears, kisses, and hugs were all in joy—an uninhibited display of love and affection.

All were enthusiastically returned by Captain Nibaw, who was also Dorjan of Harb.

Fifteen minutes after the reunited couple managed to release each other (reluctantly) from their rib-crushing embraces, Lizina had Dorjan onboard *Windrammer*. Her original intent was to give him a guided tour of her ship. The tour made it one room past the con-cabin. To Lizina's own cabin.

There she dragged Dorjan inside and locked the door behind him. A minute later (the minimum time needed to shed their clothing) they were in bed.

Neither the crew of *Misfit* nor of *Windrammer* saw its captain for the next twenty-four hours. No member of either crew voiced any objection.

Lizina's intimately probing tongue slowly withdrew from its languid duel with Dorjan's. Their lips parted. She leaned back and smiled. Her emerald eyes were agleam with life. That same life had every cell in her body tingling.

"Mmmmmmmm." Her satisfaction was manifest in that throaty purr. "Have I told you that you're good?"

Dorjan nodded while his palm tenderly caressed the warm satin of her breasts. "Three times in the past two hours. But don't stop. It builds the male ego."

"Three times! Have you been counting?" Her tone was one of mock indignation. She laughed. "Actually, it's four."

He said, "Sure." Dorjan's laughter rose in chorus with hers as he drew her to him for another kiss. "Shall we try for five?"

"Pos . . . but later. We have to talk. So much has happened since Ganesa's attack on HOME." Lizina's face sobered. "Booda! In some ways it seems that years have passed since then, Dorjan!"

Dorjan's fingertips lightly traced over her cheek. "We're together again. That's all that matters—what we have now and the future that will be ours."

Lizina's brow furrowed and her head moved from side to side on the pillow. "Things have happened to me. Things I think you should know about."

Dorjan answered with a nod.

She told him everything, beginning with Ganesa's raid on the asteroid colony and concluding with her sending *Forerunner* into the Maelstrom. She told him of the men who had used her—bought, or rather rented, her body—and the young man who had loved her. Chane, to whom she had given herself.

Dorjan listened in silence. When she was through, he nodded again.

"Well?" She stared, perplexed by his lack of reaction.

"I've already said it, Lizina. What we have now and what awaits us in the future is all that matters." He eased her to him again. "Now, are you ready to try for five?"

She replied by sliding beneath him.

Yemahl Huhleem's unspoken fantasies concerning Lizina were shattered the moment she walked into his office with Captain Nibaw. He had felt that the young man, Chane, was but a passing fancy for Lizina. But this one, this *Nibaw*, made her eyes like fiery jewels. Yemahl knew he was seeing the inner light of a woman in love.

Were I but forty years younger! Then perhaps I could give this Nibaw some solid competition.

Yemahl's wife of those forty years never entered his fantasies. In reality he would never have left her. Still, a shattered fantasy—especially one as enticing as Lizina—was a disheartening experience. So much so that the attorney never questioned Lizina's liquidation of several small, but profitable assets.

Nor did he question her decision to place the remainder of her estate into a trust. He did grin widely when she named Yemahl Huhleem as trustee of the estate.

Shattered fantasies proved easily forgotten.

"We'll need another ship to get this cargo to HOME," Dorjan said while he ran an inventory check on the latest shipment of crates that had been uplifted to Panishport.

"We have *two*!" Lizina's gaze ran over the crates filling the space station's tunnel.

Medical equipment, seed, a backup spaceship drive, crate atop crate of edutapes—all HOMEward bound.

She liked to believe that Garold Harith would have approved of the way she had invested a small portion of his wealth. Garold had possessed a certain knack for backing new ventures. The Kuzih planets were definitely that.

"I was talking about three ships—maybe *four!*" Dorjan grinned at her. "We'll have to store most of this at Barbro and make several runs to get it all to HOME."

"Sounds all right with me." She kissed him, loudly and wetly. "As long as I'm along on those runs."

Lizina stared at Chane, shocked by his announcement. "Are you sure?"

He nodded. "This HOME just isn't what I want. It's obviously right for you, as is this Captain Nibaw. I've never seen you happier, Lizina. But it's not what I want."

"Nor I." This from Hoku, looking very comfortable and right at Chane's side.

Lizina took a deep breath and nodded. She had always envisioned *Windrammer*'s whole crew onboard HOME.

"I signed on to help you, Lizina. You've no need of that help anymore. To be honest, I'm ready to get back to living my own life." Chane appeared embarrassed by his last admission. Still, his eyes remained clear and his head up.

"I understand." Lizina nodded. "Have any idea what that life is going to entail?"

Chane shrugged. "Hoku and I have talked about it. Nothing certain yet. But don't worry. I've banked the generous salary you've paid me. There's enough tucked away to give us time to make up our minds."

"Ever thought about a ship of your own?" Lizina grinned widely as an errant thought wiggled into her conscious.

Chane laughed. "Pos. But spacers *cost!*"

"This one will cost you three hops to the Barbro Transfer Station with holds filled with cargo," Lizina said. The more she thought about it, the more she liked the idea.

"What?" Chane stared at her as though she had lost her mind.

"Listen a few minutes. Chane, I'm promoting you to captain of *Windrammer*."

He listened. And ten minutes later he agreed to Lizina's outrageously generous offer. *Windrammer* was his in exchange for hauling HOME's supplies and equipment to Barbro.

After all, a spacer had room for but one captain. And *Misfit* was Lizina's ship now. The master of *Misfit* was Dorjan of Harb. That was the way she wanted it.

Two months after that cautious meeting with Captain Nibaw within the Hub Bar, *Misfit* (with Lizina beside her captain) slipped onto the Tachyon Trail on its way HOME.

22

"You aren't serious!" Dorjan's smile faded when he saw the expressions on Songan's and Varn's faces. His two friends *were* serious. "Booda! Why? HOME will be ready to launch in two days. Two days, Songan, and we'll be under weigh for the Kuzih planets!"

The tattooed giant nodded heavily. "Those two days are what forced my decision, Dorjan. HOME will be traveling in the opposite direction from Hawking."

Hawking? Dorjan stared at his friend. What had Hawking to do with . . . He remembered. He had been so caught up in preparations—and with Lizina—that he had forgotten. *The research team!*

"Yoluta—there's a possibility?"

"I don't know. I've followed the reports out of Hawking. There's still no conclusive evidence the cellular approach to memory retrieval is valid." Songan sucked at his cheeks and shrugged. "But if there is a chance, I have to try. I have to know."

Dorjan understood. He understood—damn it! Songan had to go. Had to do what he felt was required.

Kuzih—the stars! They were supposed to belong to Songan, too! And Varn!

Dorjan, confused and feeling as if his whole world had gone topsy turvy, looked at *Misfit*'s computrician.

"What can I say? I've never served a better captain or crewed onboard a ship as fine as *Misfit*. It's been good. But HOME won't be the same." Varn shrugged.

221

"Besides, this tattooed genius will be lost without someone to keep an eye on him. Genius he might be. But we Outies are slippery!"

Something rang hollow in Varn's flippant answer. But then Varnalgeran Yuw had always been an enigma to Dorjan. Yuw's past remained as shadowy now as it had been when *Misfit*'s crew had rescued him from slavers on the planet Lyon.

Dorjan didn't question him further. The choice to leave HOME was Varn's, the same as it was Songan's.

"You both know that HOME will always have a place for you."

"I'll be back." Songan smiled weakly. "I've already prepared a cassette with the coordinates of the Kuzih worlds encoded to crystal. Someday I'll slot that cassette into a SIPACUM. But first, I have to travel to Hawking."

"Who knows, I might be onboard with this ugly Harbian." Yuw grinned.

"Ships don't grow on trees!" Dorjan shook his head.

"We might have to find another Shadow Walker, but we'll get a ship." Songan glanced at his friend. "We've stolen more heavily guarded items than a spacer, old friend."

"I think the original Shadow Walker has a better plan." If these two were set on leaving, he had no intention of jaunting to Barbro Transfer Station and leaving them there as they had suggested. "*Lung T'ou* is yours. As to who will be its captain is something you'll have to argue out among yourselves."

"SotKil's ship?" A wide grin split Songan's tattooed face. "It's supposed to be a backup to *Misfit*."

Dorjan shook his head. "The Demon Cat is retired. *Misfit* doesn't need a backup. It's ready—complete with a new facelift—whenever you are. It'll need forged registration, but then both of you have done that before."

"And a new name." Varn winked at the winged

Harbian. "Something that'll suit its new captain. Something like *Rainbow Runner* or . . ."

"In the morning, Dorjan," Songan said, ignoring the Outie's forced humor.

Dorjan needed no further explanation of what his friend meant. He nodded his approval of the ship's departure. Then he reached out and threw his arms about both men, hugging them close. Dorjan was unashamed of the tears that welled in his eyes.

From a Songan-designed observation bubble Dorjan and Lizina watched *Fleet Return* easily slip through the wide corridor that had been cleared in the asteroid belt for HOME's impending departure. Man and woman held each other tightly. The goodbyes had been said and all that remained was to watch Songan and Yuw begin their journey . . . a journey that would take the two to the opposite side of the galaxy.

"They will return." Lizina looked up into the face of the man she loved. The emerald of her eyes was misted by tears.

"Songan will. When, I don't know. But he will." Dorjan hugged her closer "I can't say the same for Varn. He's an Outie, and who can guess what an Outie will do!"

"They'll be back. Both of them," Lizina said with certainty.

Dorjan merely nodded and squeezed her tightly. He felt the swell of her stomach pressed against him—his growing son. He immediately released her and stepped back, afraid he had hurt her.

Lizina smiled. "I'm pregnant, not breakable."

She pulled him to her again. Her gaze returned to the void of space beyond the bubble. *Fleet Return* was gone, now a stream of tachyons leaping the parsecs of space on a voyage that would take two friends to the limits of the galaxy's boundaries.

"Show me where we're going."

Dorjan lifted an arm and pointed directly overhead. "You can't see the Kuzih stars from here. But they're in that general direction."

"And we'll be giving them to our son." She smiled, emerald eyes flashing with pride.

"And we'll give them to our *sons* and *daughters!*"

"Sons and daughters!" Lizina grinned with delight.

Her gaze moved over the blackness of space and the distant stars. Her chest expanded with pride. The vastness that stretched around her would belong to her children. Their birthright would be the spaceways.